# GEORGIA BUDDHA

# GEORGIA BUDDHA

## STORIES

BY

## V.N. EBERT

Published by Passage Publishing



Cover design by Wide Dog



Printed in the United States of America

For information, contact support@passage.press

ISBN: 978-1-959403-98-2

Passage Publishing
www.passage.press

*In memory of my grandmother*

# CONTENTS

# SKY BURIAL

Ran his fingers through his hair he had just shaved real close. Fingers pricked over stubble and the boy felt like a monk.

His left hand remained on the wheel, held low, below the level of the dash. Repeated running his hand over what was left of his light-blonde hair and then placed his right hand back on the wheel as he took a curve. The road had devolved from paved to gravel to dirt and his wheels dug tracks in the red dirt in those parts which were bare, and decaying leaves in those parts were wooded.

Was grateful for the dry weather. Was like God giving his blessing for the task at hand and so far he could tell was only trying to do what was difficult and rightful.

Windows were rolled down and the outside air was unseasonable, uncomfortable warm and soggy humid, fighting with the air-conditioning even with it at full blast. Course, could've rolled his windows up and only been with the air-conditioning and the dying dog in the crate but that would've been another worser way of being uncomfortable.

The curve straightened out and the wheels found a rut and the truck was directed forward, wasn't new but wasn't so old as to be unpresentable. Was a good solid American truck and was paid for indirectly by the US Army. A paycheck derives first from the employer writing the check, or the big tabulating machines which ran the checks, as everything was going automated and those checks were spent by the recipients on the necessities and luxuries of life. Trees on either side of the road had grown tall and their limbs had spread, and those branches formed an archway over the road, and so he drove his truck which was a respectable vehicle for a boy making his way in the world directed by dark brown ruts under the yellowing-leafed archway.

Caught the crate in his rearview beneath the gun rack and the rifle in that rack. Inside was his dead daddy's dog. Over the blasting sound of the air-conditioning and over the dimmed sound of the inrushing air, had to slow down in the road, the ruts had slowed the truck down, boy heard the dog whimper. Sound couldn't have been so loud considering the shape the dog was in.

Boy looked at himself in the mirror to look at something else. Was a dirty ring around his neck the color of sorghum. Undid the buttons of his collar going far enough down to open his shirt to the breast. Had sweat underneath the armpits. Jeans were riding up, pinching, but he had expended what spare energy he had opening his shirt and left them to pinch.

Had been sure he would recognize that field when he came upon it even if he never had known the address. His daddy'd used to lease it, but the lease had long since expired. Dog had liked the field, daddy took the dog oftener and longer than he had him. Boy had heard dogs are sometimes liable not to make it much longer than their owner, at least, the kind of dog was attached and didn't see fit to pine and just went ahead and decided would up and join him.

Suppose this dog was in the middle of those kinds of dogs. Was still breathing like a dying organ. Couldn't say the dog could do much more than that but had a persistence like it was trying to push all the air out of its lungs and only kept breathing more air in without meaning to and having to prolong the process of dying.

Hadn't been driving the last time he'd been to where he was trying to get with his daddy's dog. Course, couldn't bring his daddy with him now, and daddy hadn't left directions behind, written somewhere they could be found. To be fair, he was not expecting any kind of writing any more than he was expecting anything from his daddy, even last words. If the county sheriff hadn't made a call to the base, would not have known his daddy was dead. Had been plenty of delay, not a soul other than the dog had been with his daddy except maybe the spirits of the already dead, if those saw fit to hang around after they was gone and boy couldn't see much point in that. Hardly would have been much to see except a dead man rotting and his dog making a mess in the house. Might have been something on which to cogitate, a man dying and still sitting in his chair while there got to be less and less of him and what was still there was putrid and corrupt, but that wouldn't seem like it could be much interest to folks was already dead.

Maybe of interest to the living, though.

Was the kind of consideration his former girlfriend had told him happened in places weren't America. That girl was a stripper turned hippie reverted back to being a stripper. She hadn't been as much fun at any of those periods as he had expected her to be. She had tried reading some and mostly didn't finish the books except the dirty ones and he ended up finishing some of the ones she left open. She told him about that kind of consideration one night after they had taken blotter acid because she said all the hippies in San Francisco took it and it made sex something else. Maybe it was true about the hippies taking it, but he hadn't found it true about sex at all. Instead, had tripped and walked across rolling green fields like a grassy sea and felt in himself like it was rushing through his blood that he was a long time ago in Ireland before the English came, and this was strange because he was Scots Irish. But had felt peaceable, perfectly peaceable, and like all things were good, even if that country was going to get occupied and blighted, because there was that grassy sea that was perfect and green and curved past the blue horizon and having existed once, would always exist in eternity.

Girl had told him when he was back from the green fields and still plenty high and not able to do much when it came to sex there was something monks in Tibet did before Tibet was Red Chinese. That when a monk died the other monks took the dead one to a butcher and the butcher dismembered the dead monk into easy-to-carry pieces. The monks carted those pieces to a hill and spread him out. Then they sat and watched while the pieces was eaten by buzzards and other carrion-eating birds. Spent the time they spent watching thinking over life and how life didn't last. Girl who was a hippie then and trying to read even if it went against her nature said they called it a sky burial.

He'd asked why she told him that and she said it was because she wanted to freak him out. He said it hadn't freaked him out. It was beautiful and she got real quiet and didn't suggest doing acid anymore after that.

Later on after he told her he was going career she'd gone on a tear about his having voluntarily made himself an instrument of the war. Was bad enough he hadn't burnt his draft card and now he was committing himself willfully. She had called him the universal soldier, which was the title of a peacenik song with a spitting-on-the-troops quality to it, and he had called her plenty more things and that had been the end of their relationship, not that he regretted the ending. Had swore off hippies and strippers before he had met her and not kept his promise to himself.

Still read the books she'd left behind. She had taken the dirty ones with her but hadn't missed them too much, and there was always the opportunity to score a Tijuana bible, but hadn't seen any other copies of the *Mahabharata* around the base.

Truck hit a rut and didn't hurt the suspension none, truck could handle plenty, but upset the crate and was a cruelty to the dog to keep on driving. Hadn't been that field so long, even before falling out with his daddy, so they didn't speak none. His daddy had started going on his own with the dog, and that didn't help the boy's sense of time and distance, how not knowing where you are going makes the journey longer. And was cruel to daddy's dog having to drag out its waiting. Boy had to do his own waiting but oughtn't put that waiting on the dog.

There was a stretch of good shoulder on the road adjacent to a low fence. Kind of fence was put up more to mark property than to ward off trespassers, didn't have no wire on it. Boy pulled his truck off there.

Beyond the fence was a field he didn't recognize but would serve even if it did have knee-high weed grass at the fence. Read in one of those books his girl left behind, monks went to places that were run down and degenerate to meditate on life and this might've been one such place.

Left the keys in the ignition and the engine and air conditioner running. Rolled the windows up to keep the cool air inside the truck. Stepped out of the truck and boots were reddened and the spit shine was ruined in the dust. Was a moment of doubt standing there with the door open and the low fence in front of him. Gathered himself and muttered under his breath and shut the door behind him, and he was committed as though he had made a contract with God instead of only telling himself this was what he ought to do. Even if his daddy had been a bastard, there was more than one way to bury him. This was one of those ways because the county had buried him another way, denying him a proper burial.

Made sure his jeans were tucked into his boots and his shirt tucked into his jeans and closed his shirt up to the neck. All was a way to prevent ticks. Exercise also burnt up a little time and that wasn't something he was averse to even if he was committed, because hell, he was only a man, weren't he.

Stepped out to that fence and could tell the field beyond had been cleared out at some point with no trees or stumps across an acre. Was bounded on three sides by trees ridden with kudzu and the fourth by that fence.

Hitched a leg over followed by the other and he was on the other side of the fence in the field. Was a low hill a short distance into the field and the grass was not growing so high on it. Hill was rounded and reminded him of a burial mound like the Indians used to make and where he supposed some are still buried. From the top could see over the trees toward more trees and the line of the horizon. The stretch of kudzu ended before reaching the horizon and at least some trees were free of it. Was a hawk circling over something already dead or soon to be.

Supposed was the nature of things how life was suffering.

But, even in suffering, there was something to be said for the act of living and here was one of those acts of living, which was doing right by his daddy. Even if his daddy had been a bastard and his dog, which hadn't done nothing wrong except love a bastard, and outlive him.

The weed grass wasn't the soft green of Ireland back sometime when his ancestors was living there and might still be. Boy had never been to Ireland and so couldn't say. Might have been the right field, where he was now situated. Would have to be lying to himself to claim he was certain this was his daddy's lease but would have to be of service how the imperfect is always the servant of the perfect.

Made his way down the field and felt the ground curving under him like the lines in grammar school, could go on forever past the end of the page rising endlessly by slow degrees, and the rest of the field was like the first part. The long part of the line that hardly rises at all and he reached his truck at the point where everything was zero, which was the center.

The back door of his truck opened by a handle, and he could only reach the handle with the front door open and so to get to his daddy's dog in the back seat he would have to open both doors. After opening the front he leaned in and turned the key in the ignition. Weren't going to need the air anymore. Only then he took the needful next motion and opened the back door and was looking through the grate of the dog crate.

Daddy's dog was still breathing and body was rising and falling shallowly and in widely spaced intervals. It was a black lab though its coat had turned closer to gray and its coat was matted where the dog had been biting and pawing at himself. That activity must have used up what energy dog had left.

Opened the mesh and dog didn't respond, not that he expected a response. Considered carrying only the crate but it had been spoilt by urine. Smell mixed with gun oil. Boy'd had to clean the rifle and had then put the dog into the crate with the oil still on his hands and so there was oil on the dog's matted fur. Had cleaned his hands after but not considered that here now the smell would be stronger.

Reached in and took his daddy's dog in his arms. Felt the dog's pulse because of how little there was left. Boy held the dog close to his chest, head lolled over the boy's arm as though dog's neck were broken. Propped his head onto his arm. Smell soaked into its coat was ammoniac.

Boy'd hoped to make only one trip but the dog was too heavy and too awkward to hold in only one arm and so he would have to leave the rifle on the rack. Left the doors open because whether they were open or closed didn't seem consequential.

Had a great fear of dropping his daddy's dog, like the fear of interrupting a church funeral. Hitched over the fence and while raising his second leg was conscious of being off-balance, of the nearness of falling. Had the thought, those same monks went to bad places to meditate, operating on the principle what might save you will probably kill you. Fear of falling like his soul responding to that fearsome insight.

Placed his daddy's dog at the crest of the hill, and dog was uncomplaining.

Went back for the rifle and gripped it with both hands and lifted it from the rack. Admired the smoothness of the barrel and maybe that girl had been right about something else because he had in his hand an excellent machine that was excellent because it was suited to its task and that task being hard was no mark against the instrument. Might have been the universal soldier because he was either born or conditioned to admire such quality and preferred to believe his soul had been born to it. Some of those monks talked like that too, that a man might be saved by becoming aligned with the action that suited his own soul and he had never regretted going career.

Chambered a round and put a spare in his pocket from the box of ammunition in the glove compartment. More to assure himself he was pragmatic and prepared for an unlikely eventuality, even if he was committing himself to something strange and thinking about monks from places he weren't from and had only heard of because he'd thought that girl looked damned fine on stage.

His daddy's dog hadn't died in the meantime which would have been gentler but then life and necessity are rarely gentle.

Said an improvised memorial over the dog, things he wouldn't have said if he thought folks could hear it. Said his daddy might have been a bastard, but he had loved his dog and his dog loved him. Dog didn't know no better, but so they might least be together now even if they was going to be born again, and so maybe their spirits would follow each other. Then did what had to be done. The shot was clean because he took good care of his rifle, respected its quality.

And then boy sat on his haunches and waited.

Thought about nothing for a long time and felt like he was back in that green and grassy sea after thinking about nothing for a long time. Flies found the dog first and that wasn't surprising even if it weren't so grand as the carrion-eating birds and some of the flies landed on him. Kept sitting on his haunches thinking of nothing. When the first crow landed on the dog was like a strange kind of deliverance.

After a time, there was a flock of birds and swarm of flies covering the dog and eating away what was left of it before sunset, and he had hardly moved. Because the mass of things around what had been his daddy's dog were shifting and changing their place constantly, the dead half of the pair was in greater motion because what was left was becoming part of the birds and the flies. And so from one perspective, by extension, dog was moving with them and from another perspective was being annihilated and from another, dog was dead and everything after being dead didn't matter so much. Although boy didn't accept that last way of looking at things, didn't know if he could reject it either, but there was a way of not holding it close to him and instead having it out at a middle distance.

He wasn't one of those monks would spend all his time meditating in an abattoir. Didn't think he would like to be one even were he given the opportunity. He had spent enough time thinking of nothing and not bothering the flies. The sun was lowering in the sky, so he finally started back to get the shovel.

Digging felt honest and rightful. Wasn't how the Tibetans managed dying but then he weren't in Tibet and his daddy and his daddy's dog weren't monks in Tibet so there was room for adjustment. Digging also takes longer than folks imagine, and it is hard work, and he dug deep. Motion rubbed his hands and opened a blister and didn't stop him but there was blood on the handle.

Used the shovel to scare away the birds but couldn't do much about the flies and he came near to retching using the shovel to pick up what was left of his daddy's dog. Wasn't picked through clean to the bone because the process had run its course earlier than that but there was bones showing. Tried to catch down vomit and gagging and holding the shovel as far from him as he might because he found his limit of what he could stomach because he was a man, weren't he, and got the remains into the hole in the hilltop.

Started shoveling dirt back into the hole and looking down was reminded of something else. Was a thing a group of monks said in Cambodia, which was next to South Vietnam. They would say something like, this condition of being dead and putrid was their fate, too, and the fate of all men, and everything could count itself alive and weren't nothing they could do to escape their fate, which was being dead.

Boy kept piling dirt and pondered. Couldn't argue the logic of it, short of Jesus coming back tomorrow and even that would be the raising of the dead, because near-enough everybody who has ever lived is now dead. And his daddy was dead. And boy would die someday because he wasn't putting too much money on Jesus, who seemed to keep His own arrival mysterious and leisurely.

But, now the dirt covered the remains and the boy thought, that is a different sort of being dead. Being in a grave. Getting a funeral of monks watching a body being eaten by birds and flies. Sure enough had been something for the boy sitting on his haunches through it. Didn't fix the part of being dead which was the act of dying, but might be that it sorted itself out through religion, or maybe it didn't, and then there wasn't nothing could be done. But was something different to this way of being dead.

Boy patted the dirt flat and had some of the weed grass that had been pulled up with the soil still mixed with it, and same weed grass would cover the hillside grave. Boy knew would like as not never be at this spot of earth again.

Left the shovel on the grave because he had no more need of it and wouldn't have wanted to keep it even if he had.

Thought of his daddy and felt oddly grateful for that girl who hadn't known a damned thing but ended up teaching something how a man's path can be revealed to him by unexpected and unknowing teachers and perhaps he in turn teaches others without intending it.

Walked down to the fence and hitched his legs over and didn't fear losing his balance this time. Took that as confirmation he had done good. Got in his truck and put the rifle back on its rack and started off again. Ran his hand over his hair that he had just shaved real close.

# GEORGIA BUDDHA

Buddy Stonewall Jackson regretted sending his oldest son to college. Especially having let his son have his own way and going off to Berkeley College in New York. Buddy'd named his oldest Robert Lee, had felt like a good solid name. Buddy's first sign of trouble was when his son made mention over Christmas vacation that he was calling himself Siddhartha.

Buddy hadn't gone to college, hadn't had any expectation or desire for being a college boy. He'd only finished high school because he'd been a football hero, a lineman and nineteen years later still had the body of a standout defensive player, and had wanted to go for a state ring.

He still wore the 1950 ring, only piece of jewelry excepting his wedding band.

When his oldest gave the news, Buddy was wearing both rings and a white double-breasted suit and sitting next to his second wife who was blonde and eleven years his junior, and who had given Buddy twin sons a month earlier. They were the sixth and seventh children, and the sixth and seventh sons, she'd given him in eight years of marriage. Buddy in his gratitude had bought her the mink coat and fox stole which she was wearing at the dining table, and was going to give her a pair of diamond earrings and another honeymoon skiing in Colorado without the children for Christmas.

Buddy'd leaned over his desert of candied yams to close the gap between himself and his son and proceeded to bellow loud enough to terrify the domestics in starched collars stationed at the corners of the room and rattle the glass chandelier which Buddy had bought in Paris.

"What crap in the risen Christ you just tell me?"

His oldest, who had never been a football player and looked scrawny, almost stooped compared to Buddy's weight-trained shoulders, his five-eight feet a rail-thin halfhearted imitation of Buddy's six-four massive figure, raised his voice. He didn't have Buddy's lungs, which had started out strong and gotten stronger after a football-crazy planter had graduated Buddy from field hand to overseer immediately out of high school. The boy had to try to lower his pitch, using that unaccented English he'd acquired.

"I said that I'm going by Siddhartha."

Buddy ordered a domestic, none in particular, to get him a sheet of paper and a pen without breaking eye contact with his son.

"Boy, I ain't certain what you're saying, but I am certain that that ain't your name."

His son shrugged beneath the greasy, long hair which Buddy thought made him look like a faggot, a fact over which Buddy'd restrained himself from commenting unduly.

"It's the name I'm going by."

Buddy's second wife gave him a peck on the cheek and excused herself, saying quietly that she was going to look in on the children. Buddy out of habit gave her something between a pat and a slap on the ass as she walked away and watched his son's lips curl.

One of the domestics hurried back into the dining room, not breaking stride in his bow to Buddy's second wife on her way out, crossed the room and put the pen and paper down in front of Buddy's son on the tablecloth which smelt like it had been pulled out of a dryer and ironed an hour before supper. His son wrote down his new name, handed it to the domestic, who rushed without running and handed it to Buddy. Buddy moved his lips as he read the name, didn't find that it helped.

"Crap."

Buddy wondered why he hadn't put his son to work. It didn't have to be something involving much money, even clerking at the bank Buddy owned the controlling stock in. Hell, if his son was going to cling onto a deferment and stay out of the war, why not Ole Miss where no boy ever came home with this sort of problem? Buddy hadn't been a drinking man, which likely'd helped with his doing so well for himself. Right then with his son, he wanted to take a slug of straight whisky.

"Son, this ain't a name."

Buddy liked to brag he'd done so well. He'd say, I went from being worked like a nigger to working a damned lot of folks like niggers. Buddy'd lived in a dogtrot shack provided by the planter who'd been working him all through high school. Buddy's parents had died young, momma had always been malarial, sickly, passed his freshman year. His pappy died from feeling sorry for himself Buddy's sophomore year.

Buddy was then joined by his first wife, who he'd married two months after the boozy party for winning state, wherein he'd felt like a stud. Her ma and pa hadn't said a word to her after getting her and Buddy married.

Buddy had been living in a shotgun shack with his shotgun bride when his first son was born.

Buddy was a rich man by the time his son was six and his first wife was dying.

Buddy was a millionaire by the time his son was nine and his first wife was buried.

Buddy had a second wife and a second son before his oldest was eleven.

After the second son, Buddy'd noticed that he and his first weren't talking so much. He had thought it was grief. After a time, Buddy adjusted himself to a distance between himself and his oldest, thought his son had a hard shell. Having plenty of money and a son who didn't seem to like living in Georgia much, Buddy asked him on his twelfth birthday if he'd prefer a boarding school. His son had said yes sir, and Buddy'd hugged him before leaving him on the plane bound for an expensive school in the Tidewater.

That night, at dinner, Buddy kept on about the new name. After some more shouting, he heard that it was from a book by a man with the Kraut-sounding name of Hermann Hesse, which his son also wrote down on a piece of paper, after assuring Buddy that the man was Swiss, the better kind of German.

After dinner and the argument ended, his oldest gone into a guest bedroom to sulk, Buddy read to his twins in their nursery, minstreling through Uncle Remus. Buddy liked narrating as the old house nigger, and his boys who were old enough to understand followed real close and hated how they did every night when Buddy put down the weathered copy and kept the voice as he told them, "Wah ha' to be keepin' on ta-marrah." Gave each a kiss on a clean and powdered forehead, told "ga-night" with his eyes bugged out and showing his tongue which seemed pinker than at other times, and left them to the ministration of mammies, or, for the youngest, the white and expensive wet nurses.

Found his second wife on the master bedroom gallery looking out onto the hothouse where gardeners grew orchids and the heated swimming pool, with winter honeysuckle reaching over the wood balustrade. She'd changed out of the furs into a slip of a nightgown that Buddy liked her wearing, red panties and pink nipples and gooseflesh begging for Buddy to warm her up showing through the chiffon. Rode his hands on her wide hips which Buddy had known'd be fine for bearing children the first time he'd looked her over, Buddy being a healthy man with a healthy appetite that was at first meeting her.

She smiled at him, revealing those teeth which were straighter than the slightly buck teeth which had afflicted Buddy's first wife, and which she'd always hated.

Now, Buddy held his second wife, rocked with her on a wide swinging chair, scratched his hard-on and pulled her onto his lap, weren't worried about her getting any bullshit into her head about being on top, talked dirty to her because she still blushed when he did. Course, now she was warm, excitedly flushing instead of virgin modesty. Gripped his hand with its championship ring and wedding band around hers with her wedding ring, hers being a substantial diamond set with emeralds.

Buddy'd talked a little dirty to her while they was first going together, wasn't a damn long time, but the first night he'd gone on a blue tear was their wedding night, the night after their courthouse marriage with her Episcopalian parents still reeling from her dropping out of high school, getting hitched to a man that their small set, with its blue-blooded gentility, had never stopped considering an uppity cracker. Buddy didn't mind, seeing as most of that set owed him money and sucked his ass like they was field niggers when it came to renegotiating the terms of their loans. Her folks had done their best to make a cold fish out of his girl, but Buddy'd known after first talking her up that he'd found a filly was hot to trot and he had decided real quick, if she was going to get herself into trouble otherwise, he might as well be the man who made an honest woman out of her. Buddy liked to think that he'd put Rafe, their first son together, inside his second wife that very first night.

Sitting on his porch, Buddy held her chin and puckered her lips by applying pressure, used his tongue to open her teeth, stuck it down her throat and she was panting and begging how he liked when he gave her a sloppy lick on the cheek. Being that she was ready, and Buddy'd been horny since the day his balls had dropped between his legs, he got her in bed and out of the slip and panties, didn't even take off his hand-tooled boots or the Swiss watch he'd bought in France with its wide white dial, before mounting her like she was in heat for the first time since the twins. She unlaced Buddy's boots after, and he took them off while she took her turn washing herself at the bidet which Buddy'd had installed after coming back from Paris, where the first time he'd seen one, had pissed in it thinking it was a peculiar urinal. After Buddy'd washed and taken off his suit and everything else, he held her in bed, under covers, smelling of daily washing and pressing by domestics, both sinking in the feather mattress like they were conspicuous otherwise and thought huddling down together was sexy.

Buddy knew he ought to be cooling on his second wife, but was still falling in bed with her real easy and goddamn'd never been seriously tempted to get a woman in town. When Buddy was in his feather bed with his blue-blooded wife who he'd corrupted to be a real fine lay, knowing with her streak she'd have another child in her by New Year's, knowing all those sons were in the nursery being looked over by women he could pay without thinking about the money, even the white girls he couldn't chew and cuss out quite so thoroughly when they was being worthless and who saved his wife from having to suckle, dozing in an air-conditioned plantation mansion he'd built without taking on debt, Buddy felt he'd made himself a happy man.

Now, Buddy wasn't letting his oldest son Robert Lee dirty that feeling.

About a week later, right before Christmas, Buddy's son left. Both kept themselves quiet on the drive to the airport, and were civil enough to exchange gifts sitting in the car. His son gave him a thumbed-through copy of *Siddhartha* as a present. Buddy gave his son a record, *Whipped Cream & Other Delights*, as Buddy liked the music and loved the cover, not finding a pretty woman wearing nothing but whipped cream exactly unpleasant. Buddy was reassured by his son smiling when he saw the cover, wouldn't have minded a whistle but it was at least some sign of hot-bloodedness.

Buddy read *Siddhartha* during the flight out to the skiing vacation in Colorado. The copy was water-damaged and smelled of mold, but Buddy never considered buying a copy without the damage and the smell. Once in Colorado, Buddy reread *Siddhartha* again. Once he'd gotten his head around it, he started thinking his son was both being strange and damned arrogant taking that name.

Back home, Buddy joined a lending library for the first time in his life, and having asked around for books about California, found a copy of *The Electric Kool-Aid Acid Test*, which reported on Ken Kesey, LSD, and the Grateful Dead.

After he'd finished that book, Buddy mail-ordered the LP *The Grateful Dead*, and in addition he ordered Big Brother and the Holding Company's *Cheap Thrills* because the title caught his attention and the cover wasn't reproduced in the catalog.

Buddy hid the albums in his home office when they arrived. His face had flushed when he'd seen the covers. Buddy sent his second wife and children, accompanied by domestics and mammies to keep the whole circus under control, out to a Friday dinner and a double feature. Buddy told his second wife and the children old enough to listen that he had calls to make and work to get done, and gave the remaining domestics a night off. He played the albums through after they'd all left.

Buddy liked Janis Joplin, Southern girl with lung power and a scratchy voice on *Cheap Thrills*.

Buddy started ordering music in substantial quantities, got sick of waiting for the next to arrive.

Buddy also desperately needed to get his oldest out of that college and back south. But then, the boy halfway obliged without Buddy asking. Immediately into the new semester, he dropped out and packed up to a hippie commune, though he only communicated the news three months later in an overdue letter signed Siddhartha. To Buddy's mixed relief, was in Tennessee. South, yes, college, no, but that was acceptable. But him being on a commune, well, that was worrisome.

A week after getting the letter, Buddy's boots slogged through the mud, stepping out of his Cadillac in Tennessee. It was March and temperatures were depressed, so it was cold mud. He'd stopped a ways off from the single building which looked like a cabin, parking next to a psychedelic VW bus with California tags and which looked worse for wear.

Buddy'd reached the settlement by an unpaved road, was bordered by two cleared fields with a line of trees behind. Buddy had expected a smoothly sloping Appalachia, would've been a better place for running off to. Hadn't expected the commune would look and, in the absence of any form of domestic animal life, in its lack of animal manure and the missing presences of pecking and ruminating, sound and smell so much like an abandoned farm. Had he known about the mud, wouldn't have had his boots shined after searching through the directory by the pay phone in the one diner in town. He'd been trying to find a number to call ahead, to give some advanced warning, though the operator had been worthless. Had sent a reply letter instead and wrote in it the day he was coming up, but Buddy didn't particularly trust that his son would've gotten the letter. Or opened it if he'd received it.

Buddy had a 33 RPM *Safe as Milk* double album under his arm. Thought it might make a peacemaking present, or something he can only call different in the way it sounded like

Howlin' Wolf if Howlin' Wolf had had a stroke and started listening to instrumental music beamed in by aliens. Buddy found he liked it after the fourth listen, thought his son might not've listened to it even once already.

Buddy slicked back his hair in the morning, but was still clearly getting longer, and even if he was keeping his newly cultivated goatee neatly trimmed it still gave him a long-haired look. A girl with brunette hair down to her waist and a headband with a peace sign called to Buddy from the neighboring field, made her way over to him when he stopped slogging. Was in work clothes, Levi's suspenders and a plaid shirt. Saw that she was barefoot, might've helped with her time even if it showed an ignorance of hookworm. She pointed to Buddy's Cadillac from the other side of the fence separating them.

"Man, I don't think you're in the right place," she said.

Judging by her accent neither was she.

"Sister, ain't exactly for you to judge. I'm looking for a boy from Georgia by way of New York, might be going by Siddhartha, if he's gotten his head back on straight he's going by Robert or one of its derivations."

The girl adjusted a strap of her muddy overalls. She wore poor man's clothes like she was born with money.

"You must be his old man. You might want to get in that Cadillac car and get back to your digs."

Buddy'd been driving for hours, got into town late, too late to come out to the commune directly. He'd slept in a fleabag of a motel the night before.

"Whatever you know about the matter, you don't know a damned thing, so point my way to him if you're willing and if you ain't, sister, go fuck yourself."

She didn't seem bothered by the cussing.

"He should be inside the main building. Well, the only building. Weather's so bad, not much else to do."

"Except strolling through mud."

She smiled at that, had a nice smile, straight toothed and dentisted.

"Man, I didn't hassle you."

Buddy thanked her, and started trudging toward what was the main building by default. Wondered how well these folks would handle summertime heat, and how exactly they was going to feed themselves. But, was a concern for the future survivors of rural living, and Buddy expected somebody'd get a telephone call through to a rich daddy before too many bodies been buried.

The by-default main building looked so damned much like a log cabin that Buddy thought it must not've been a log cabin. Who in their fucking right mind would willingly move from someplace which wasn't a log cabin to someplace which was a log cabin? Christ, they'd be back to using a goddamned shithouse instead of a flush toilet. He turned back, pointed with his free hand.

"All of y'all live out here?"

The girl hadn't moved from where he'd left her. "You mean all of us live squashed together in that one little place? Got something like a nudie picture in your head?"

Buddy had sat through exactly one nudie picture in his life. It had been in a makeshift theater, essentially a tent with a film projector and an improvised screen outside of town limits. Buddy's first wife was almost three years into dying by then, and he'd been depressed and dispirited and blue-balled. None of which had been helped by the picture.

"Now you're hassling me. I weren't inquiring whether y'all were living in sin, worldly enough to assume it, and I meant just the first part of that."

The girl walked up to Buddy, hopped the fence separating them. "Nothing wrong with a little prurient interest. We get some folks come out here, think it's a sex-thing, one long orgy, find out we aren't prudes but we aren't that loose either."

She had a plain face but blue eyes like where water along the seashore deepens and changes to ocean. Buddy thought they made her, if not pretty, at least striking. She pointed to the album. Buddy showed it to her.

"For my boy."

She glanced at the cover.

"We have a record player, but it's mostly psychedelic. The folkies are on the way out. My digging jazz gets me dirty looks. And I don't think Sid'd like something, I haven't heard of that one but it looks like a drag."

"It ain't, it comes from an outfit calling itself Buddah Records. Can't be a drag. And Sid, that what my boy going by now?"

She pursed her lips, which could've used lipstick. She had a sun-drenched complexion. Buddy's taste in women's complexion ran conservative, preferred a girl with skin like cream. His second wife had skin like that, first wife hadn't.

"Coming from you, Sid will think it's a drag. Sid for Siddhartha." She pointed to the Cadillac. "What exactly do you do? Sid talks like you make a living off the pain and suffering of others, something heavy. You got the car for it."

Buddy spat like he had a chaw against his cheek. He'd quit chewing when his first wife let on that she was sick, cause she hated how it yellowed his teeth and gums. She said it was like his teeth were rotting too, but he'd kept the habit of spitting.

"Made my money as a planter. Now, I've got the acreage, invested what grew on it. Blue-chips and factories get better returns."

Buddy thought she'd turned a little green at his confirming he was a rich man, and being both a planter and a capitalist. The Man, squared. Wait till she found out he used to be an overseer, might start screeching. She started walking toward the main building, Buddy following.

"You don't talk like a planter," she said.

Buddy knew that was a way of saying, you sound like a goddamned redneck. He might've explained how he and his first wife and infant son had once lived worse than white trash. Buddy would never eat squirrel or rabbit or deer again and, hell, Buddy bragged that he'd lived worse than the niggers he was overseeing.

With this girl, would have to be polite. Nigras he was overseeing.

Buddy'd saved every penny to buy land from the planter he was overseeing for and who in addition to being football crazy was loose with his money and being driven to sell his property piecemeal. When that land started paying off, Buddy used that money to buy more land, until after five years he could sit down on the gallery of the antebellum mansion and offer to buy the planter out. After that, hell, that was making money while having money, which is a much simpler prospect than making money without having it, and Buddy had found he'd a talent for making money.

Usually, that story impressed people. Buddy had told it, expanded on it, never had to truly embellish it, traded on it, and felt good about himself on it, to every one of his cronies, employees, and croppers, and had moved from lusting to loving his second wife when she told him that she liked hearing the story.

With this girl, he doubted that the story'd go over so well. And his usual way of capping it off—Just takes balls and will to make something of yourself, and, without being crude, it's been said of me that I'm thickheaded—wouldn't likely impress her much.

So, saved the breath.

"That's cause I made myself one," he said.

His son took the album when they found him. Buddy imagined he could handle calling him Sid even if he'd have preferred Rob or Bob. Looked it over without sliding out either of the records, and threw it on top a pile, the cover sleeves irregular like pages with uncut edges. Were plenty of records, hardly any books. Seemed wrong, college boys and co-eds not having books. Didn't even take *Life*.

Buddy wouldn't have minded more books around, brought a copy of *Zen and Japanese Culture* with him. Buddy didn't like to think about having gone from Krauts to Nips, lying on the passenger seat of the Cadillac, but found it made for heavy reading and wasn't certain that his son'd respond well to his reading it.

Sid's hair was curling, should've combed it if he wasn't going to cut it. Unwashed, too, greasy, and the building itself smelled like cigarette smoke and grass. Buddy's lungs were burning, and his son's skin had aged, the smoke was doing him no favors, making him leathery. Buddy had softened since he'd gotten rich, the elastic had come back to his skin. His son wasn't working to death, but was aging like he was.

Buddy found himself thinking that he wore his hair better long than did his son. Wore work on himself better too, liked to imagine that in his poverty he'd smelled like sweat and toil instead of something decadent like marijuana.

"Buddy," his son said, "why'd you come here?"

Hearing his son address him by his given name felt like a punch in the stomach. Sounded so damned spiteful how he said it, name which was also an endearment. Buddy'd always liked that his name made people sound well inclined toward him.

"Well, son, I wanted to talk things over with you some."

His son walked past Buddy, toward the table which was piled high with store-bought food, bottles of cheap wine being passed around the rest of the communalists. Buddy'd refrained from even a comment about drinking before noon. His son took a bottle, took a slug, passed it to the girl who called herself Turquoise and who Buddy'd walked with and who'd introduced him to the whole crew as his son wouldn't. She didn't offer to Buddy, and he didn't request.

"We've already talked," he said. "Anything else you might've said in a letter."

Buddy felt rage gathering so deep that it was starting in his balls and working its way up. His oldest must not've even opened the letter, not even remembered Buddy'd sent it. Hands were clenching, his massive shoulders were tensing, and he was half-wondering how many of the longhairs he could take before force of numbers counted against him. Goddammit, hadn't whupped his son since he was little and now Buddy was regretting that omission almost as much as he was sending him off to college. None of them, three-quarters boys and the rest girls, excepting his son, was paying him any attention, like a strategy to keep him out of consciousness and out of existence. Hell, his son was barely paying him attention.

"Boy—I mean, son—why don't we talk outside? These folks don't want us interrupting their, well—is this breakfast or is it dinner?—either way, their meal."

His son took another swig from a different bottle making the rounds. Handed it on.

"They don't seem to mind."

Course they didn't, was part of the plan, Operation Buddy Freak-Out. Operation Drive Out The Motherfucker, the file-folder's title red block capitals triple underlined in red for good measure. Buddy was half wondering if most of the crew weren't on acid or, seeing how calm they was, had been smoking grass already, just to unnerve him more. Course, rage can work like speed, and Buddy was hoping that his rage might be a cleaner high than Benzedrine instead of something messy which ended with him thrashing his son half to death.

"Son, I think you got it wrong."

"What my friends call me, Buddy."

Tried breathing regular, sounded like bellows in a forge but he was breathing instead of shouting.

"Boy, instead of Buddy, might go with something else. For instance, when you ain't around, my girl and the boys've preferred calling me Big Daddy," he said.

"That woman gave you that corny moniker, Buddy?"

"His momma took to it, but, actually, was Rafe, he started calling me that."

"Rafael start calling you that? Think he was just working on you. Get your ego up."

"Crap, if you'd talked to Rafe more than a damn sentence in years, you'd know just how much he hates you calling him by his full name. Only let his mamma name him that on the condition I could call him something else. And, boy, seeing as Rafe's my oldest son who'll speak to me genially, might forgive me for mentioning him positively."

"Think he looks like you?"

Buddy knew, and he knew his son knew, that all his sons by his second wife took after Buddy. Full faces, heavy and wide builds. Blue eyes, like Buddy and his second wife. His oldest had brown eyes. His momma'd had brown eyes.

"Looks like his momma had a child by me."

"She doesn't seem to be contributing much. Seems appropriate considering that she doesn't do much except spend you into the poorhouse."

Buddy felt like Brer Rabbit hitting the Tar Baby, striking with his hands and when those got stuck in the sticky tar kicking with his feet and when those got stuck head butting the impudent bastard and getting his head stuck for his trouble.

"Boy, don't speak ill of my girl. She's been a good wife to me, and she ain't hurting your inheritance any."

His son wandered over to the record player, eyed the album Buddy'd given him.

"She groove to this?"

"She don't much like it."

"Seeing she's near enough to my age, can't imagine her liking hillbilly. Bet she's a rock-and-roll girl, can see her having a good time at a concert. Wearing something expensive and skimpy. I'll give it to her. I don't know how she keeps her figure after carrying all those sons but she's still a fox."

"She swims, two hours a day. Eats like a bird when she ain't with child, doesn't go on a binge when she is, how she keeps her figure. And she ain't spending me into the ground. She don't got a bank account, her name ain't on mine. Lives on a cash allowance. So, if this is you being worried about the state of your inheritance, she ain't dented it."

Buddy didn't think that his son was worried about his inheritance. If anything, he seemed disconcertingly uninterested in Buddy's estate. But, his son seemed intent on hinting that Buddy's second wife was a slut, and if that was what his son was saying, Buddy would be honor bound to break his son's back so he never got up again.

Turquoise spoke up for him. "You keep your wife on an allowance? She give you hell about that?"

Buddy half-turned to her and laughed in spite of being angry.

"My girl giving me hell? She don't have the meanness in her to grab me by the balls."

Buddy's son coughed and made it sound disgusted.

"Last time, you said that she's the kind of girl scratches her man's balls instead, and then that after you'd broken the virginity on your wedding night you spent your honeymoon learning her to think with what's between her legs. That she'd never heard of going around the world before her wedding night but she was making the trip plenty often now."

"Crap, boy, you must've been snooping around. That ain't something I ever told you."

Turquoise was dead pale after that, and the rest of the hippies were so stunned the bottles had stopped making the rounds. Operation Buddy Freak-Out had freaked the hippies out. Buddy'd never been a prude himself, but could understand the conversation must've hit the limits of sexual expression for this crew. His son didn't notice he'd lost his home field.

"You were with some of your cronies, bragging about the girl you'd gotten yourself," his son said.

"You oughtn't have heard that. Should've been wherever you was supposed to be, but I don't feel good about that."

"So, what was I supposed to hear, considering how you was explaining sex?"

Buddy was genuinely mystified. Must've been right after his second marriage, Buddy had stopped having his crew over to his place. He still bragged over his girl, and now the sons she'd given him, but was now in the habit of sitting outside the courthouse instead, his crew stationed around him in the morning, before the heat during summertime settled, or, when he started to get plain bored in wintertime, he took it inside the temperature-controlled offices of one of his enterprises in town.

"What I tell you," Buddy said, "besides explaining what laying a girl involves?"

His son had the complexion of a plum, cheeks puffed and purpling.

"What you said about the kind of girl I should have?"

Buddy took a moment whether he'd first told his son to try and start off with a virgin so neither'd have an idea what they was doing, or something else, remembered the something else.

"Boy, I hold by the advice I gave you. You get a girl pregnant, better be the girl you're comfortable spending the rest of your life with."

"Mamma that way?"

Buddy took a moment to compose himself, because after a brief spell of holding a conversation without desiring to commit filicide, he'd gotten used to that sort of conversation. Tried breathing again, thinking how to present the wisdom of his relative old age even if he wasn't yet thirty-six.

"I'm speaking from experience."

"You know that she was the right girl when you married her?"

"I didn't know, it was a damned sudden thing, but I was lucky and made a good marriage."

That seemed to satisfy his son, though likely because he wasn't willing to attack his own mamma. His son lost his purple, turned yellow, Buddy could smell the sweat off of him, or maybe it was Buddy sweating or both of them sweating, mixing with the damned vile smoke.

His son knelt down, parsed through the albums, pulled out a Coltrane album. *Ascension*. Buddy doubted that his son was a jazz freak. Must've been Turquoise's. When his son held the album out to Buddy and said: "You think this cover makes him look like MLK?" Buddy let out a deep breath. His son was going to go after him about integration. Thank fucking Christ.

"How was it you felt about the Freedom Riders? How'd sit-ins strike you?"

Buddy tried not to start crying in relief.

"Same way I felt about that preacher-man King. Think I usually phrased it something like, they was all radicals come to stir up trouble with our niggers."

His son, triumphantly jaundiced, passed by to stand at the head of the table, keeping the album cover—which did look a little bit like MLK holding a saxophone—facing Buddy. The whole crew of the commune behind him looked like Buddy had just put on Klan robes and announced he'd been the chief strategist for George Wallace. Buddy'd never been in the Klan, though his Cadillac did have a "Stand Up For America With Wallace" bumper sticker.

"You usually said more than that. Visiting home from that academy you shipped me to, I think you spent the time you weren't pawing at your girl ranting about, I remember you started to like calling them goddamned commie nigger sons of bitches. You had to have your wind up to get all that out in one breath."

"Boy, don't expect to convince you. Don't expect you to move me to tears."

"Are you still sitting on the board of that school?"

Buddy had in 1964 donated the lion's share of funds required to build the private grade school, in addition to providing the property. Sent all his children there when they was old enough, all holy terrors for their teachers but seeing as they still knew to respect their Big Daddy he liked that they was high-spirited. Tended to be the loudest member of the board of directors, rest were old college boys, local gentry, lawyers and doctors who lacked Buddy's direct style. Buddy frankly still thought was funny, his having never made better than a B in his life outside of physical education class and now he was running a school. Every boy took the equivalent of two physical education classes a semester.

"Boy, the school's every bit as fine as the one you attended, and more than a little bit cheaper. Even got a number of scholarship students, redneck boys doing real well."

"Any Negroes?"

Buddy hadn't gone through the trouble of building a segregation academy for the sake of having nigger students.

"There ain't. But, besides there not having been any at your boarding school, might want to look around. I ain't seen a black face since I drove in, so might want to start keeping some around before going and accusing me of something you ain't innocent of yourself. Crap, seeing as I've hardly spent a day in Georgia without at least interacting with one, I might be coming out ahead of you."

His son jumped from sickly yellow all the way to an ashen, pale fury. "Don't turn this goddamned around. It's not the same damned thing, you goddamned know it. You aren't bullshitting your way out of this."

"Well, we got our own opinions. Seeing years ain't changed either of our minds, might let the Negro question alone for a spell, talk about something of more immediate interest, namely, you getting back into college."

His son was slack-jawed. First time his face was loose.

"That what you're here about?"

"Son, I'm perplexed at how we didn't get down to nut cutting sooner."

Buddy pointed to the door, told his son, ought to go out. His son walked out ahead of him, left the album he'd made into a protest album on the communal and stunned dining table so that Coltrane stared up at the ceiling.

The view outside wasn't much improved, dismal fields and rotting fence posts strung with rusting chicken wire not looking better in harsher sunlight which still hadn't dried out the mud or raised the temperature to something comfortable. The cabin behind wasn't much better, must've been robbed blind by some hillbilly happy to dump the property in city-boys' laps.

Buddy stepped out into the mud, tried to put his hand on his son's shoulder, who jumped away like a track star.

"Boy, unless your opinion of the armed forces has dramatically improved or you got a 4-F designation you've neglected telling me about, there's a real damned good reason for you to be in school."

His son turned to face Buddy, his expression flat and dismal like the field behind him.

"If it happens, there's Canada, there's serving. More than you did."

Buddy held out his hands, his arms wide, championship ring catching the sun.

"I was married and you was a part of the family. Otherwise I'd have served in Korea, would've been better work than what I was doing." Buddy's classmates had died in Korea. Buddy hadn't, was aware of his never having gone, but still didn't care much for the loudmouthed pacifism of certain members of his son's generation. "But, crap, if you're willing, worse things than going into the military."

His son started walking back to the cabin, Buddy caught him by the arm as he passed.

"Why you leaving?"

"Nothing much to say about the draft. It happens, it happens."

Buddy recognized that his son sounded Buddhist. Supposed he could accept that his son maybe didn't know what he was doing but that his son was still committed to letting events settle out. His son broke loose of Buddy's grip because Buddy loosened his grip as his son moved away. Almost reached the door before he stood stock still. Started shaking thirty seconds into standing. Turned jerkily around, facing Buddy.

"Why did you marry that girl?" he said. Eyes were dulled, his hair so greasy it wasn't moving at the same rate as his head as it shook.

Buddy tried keeping his voice even, reasonable. "Boy, I'd been married since I was seventeen, I'd gotten so that I liked being married. What would you want? Me being not even twenty-seven and a committed widower for the rest of my life?"

"Why did you marry that girl?"

"You don't want to keep going down this road."

"Why'd you go with her and marry her when I was off at camp? Why'd you only introduce me to her when she was already your wife and pregnant with the sort of son who would call you Big Daddy?"

Buddy hadn't been able to do much with his son on his own, the months after his wife had passed. She hadn't wanted Robert to see much of her, how she was toward the end. Buddy, after he'd finished any work he could think to do or talking with the latest specialist with coke-bottle glasses and an expensive degree and no goddamn idea, staying by her in a closed bedroom with stale sickly air or on the gallery where she was wrapped in blankets no matter how miserably humid, would never tell his son that his mamma hadn't thought he could handle watching her die. But this made it hard for Buddy to be around him after. So when the school year ended, summer camp had been convenient. Buddy had happened to meet a pretty high school girl the week before sending his son off, hadn't felt that his son ought to know, hadn't expected that he'd go crazy for her as quick as he did.

All that meant Buddy was sick of being blamed.

"Ain't certain if you want me to say something honest. Say that she's sexy and, crap, that she's got as big an appetite for it as I do? That make you feel better, boy? That she's a great lay, that she goes at it like a minx? You think I ought to feel like I got a raw deal, that I got a wife who goddammit likes giving me a good time and gives me sons who answer me with sir and call me Big Daddy?"

Buddy's son looked like a mortar had fallen out of a clear sky, and where there'd been a squad of men, there was now a hole in the ground with an errant arm and mismatched leg hanging over the rim.

"A teenager with clear skin and blonde hair," he said. "Makes me want to puke, you just wanting mamma to die already so's you could keep a better woman."

If Buddy hadn't swung wild, let his punch miss by a hair, he'd have broken his son's jaw. His son jabbed after, but he'd never bothered to learn how to fight. Buddy blocked with his left, impact was harder on his son than Buddy, could have broken his wrist. Instead, he grabbed his son by the collar, yanked him up, and shoved him against the cabin. Felt the collision traveling through his son's body, head banged against a log.

Buddy held him like that, his son had gone rag-doll limp. No fight in him. Buddy had the unwelcome thought that he wasn't raising Rafe and the rest of his sons to be such goddamned sissies. Let his son down, dropped him, but his legs didn't hold him up and he crumpled down.

Buddy was standing over him. Aware how much bigger he was, didn't feel bad for being big. Felt pity for his son being so soft, and pity was mixing with disgust.

"Crap. Son, goddammit. Wasn't how this was supposed to go. But, crap."

Buddy was looking down at his son. Was looking at nothing. None his buddies had come out, in spite the noise. Shit friends on top of everything else.

"Would me marrying a brunette with acne or a dog of a schoolmarm have been better? Boy, I took care of your mamma. All through her sickness, her sickness rotting her out. It got to be that the rot smelled on her, like her insides were putrid and seeping out of her."

His son wasn't looking at him, and Buddy's vision was going red and his shouting was bellowing out from deep in him.

"I ain't ashamed to say that on her last day, when we both knew it was her last day, I was relieved. Because we was both relieved. She felt like there were things, wasps stinging or rats chewing with sharp teeth, all brawling inside of her. She didn't want any more of that. I didn't want more of that. When she died, it hurt me with a sharp pain, not the aching weight that had been with me when she was living but like my arm had been mangled in a gin."

Buddy's voice was hoarsening.

"But there was relief also, and as that sharp pain dulled that relief came more and more into focus. I was going to keep living, is all any of us have and it ain't going to last long, and part of living was going to be with a pretty woman in my bed and children on the way."

His son looked so damn much like a teddy bear with its stuffing ripped out.

"Robert, how long've you hated me?" Buddy said.

This put some spine in him.

"Since the day she died."

Buddy might've slammed his fist into his son's face. Kept going until it would be a bloody mass, stepped back. Like there was no air in his lungs.

"Why?"

"Because you worked while she died. Because you were so goddamned driving to make some damned money that you didn't notice that she was getting sick. I could've told you she was sick, I did tell you that she was getting sick, and you didn't believe she was."

Buddy stomped his boot into the damn sucking mud, the sound like popping an eardrum.

"She said she was feeling under the weather," Buddy said. "Boy, you ever feel under the weather? Under the weather usually means dead on your feet, it ever meant cancer coming from you? Told her she could go to a doctor if she wanted. She didn't. I didn't push her, because I thought she knew best how to handle herself."

"You'd not been working eighteen-hour days, already a filthy rich man and trying to be a damned multimillionaire, you'd have known better."

"Boy, spoiled you goddamn rotten. You want to be living in a dogtrot with a rusted tin roof? Cause if I weren't the kind of man I am, I weren't pushing and driving all those years, that's where you'd be boy, you'd be right there with me. Remember living like that, before I bought the mansion, before I built your mamma a new mansion because she wanted central air and a heated swimming pool and a double staircase like *Gone with the Wind* and everything else she wanted? You think anybody got to be a millionaire by being relaxed?"

"Could've been less."

"That's what folks say who've had money for a long-damned time. What rich boys who don't have children, don't have to think about giving them a comfortable future, what boys who could turn down college like they was entitled to it think living is like."

His son pointed right at Buddy.

"The Buddha says life is suffering. The only way to end suffering is to stop being attached to things."

Buddy didn't give much of a damn what a fat man who'd been born a prince had said.

"Book I read, Buddha didn't go hungry either," Buddy said. "Books I read, cause I read more than just the one you threw at me, Buddha sucked ass too, got money from plenty of rich men, promised them it'd reflect well on them. Almost buying into heaven. Buddha sold indulgences like the Catholics."

Buddy's son looked so damn surprised at him having read about the Buddha, looked as if he'd shit himself.

"Boy, takes rich men to subsidize holy men," Buddy said. "Hell, Jesus Christ had rich women following behind him. So don't act like you're better than me cause you're spending my money trying to find your soul and way in life."

Buddy thumped his chest.

"I got my way. Got a loving wife, got children I'm proud of, would like you to be one of them. I ain't dwelling in the past. Boy, you got to get over being unhappy, cause there's being trapped in life and there's punching and driving through it. Got to have goddamned balls and a strong back to make a hard world an easy one. Crap, got to have the will to be more than a piece of trash wallowing in poverty and ignorance."

His son's mouth tightened, exacerbating the lines which he was too young for. Looked to be thinking something over, behind those brown eyes which looked like a woman's almost a decade gone. "That doesn't … sound right."

"It's the goddamned truth. Can take it how you like. Man I'm reading, said this is the—called it the—how'd he say it? The golden lotus world, even if it's full of pain and misery it's still got that title. That much going for it. Things gone better, I'd have asked you about what the man might've meant, but I think, well, think I might know something more about it than you do."

His son's eyes looked like his momma's during her sickness.

"With your hair like that," he said, "it's got to be that I don't recognize you."

Buddy shrugged his weight-trained shoulders and spat. Looking down at his son, Buddy stopped holding onto the worry about his oldest.

# EUMENIDES COUNTY

Patrick parked the beat-up car with an empty fuel gauge. He and MaryAnn had been near to conking out. Diner was a rough, cheap operation off a dying county road far enough removed from the new interstate.

"I went to Chicago to get away from places like this," MaryAnn said.

Collection of trucks that were much repaired and a single shiny Cadillac.

"Might take that one," Patrick said. "Drive the rest of the way in style."

"Got to eat first," MaryAnn said. She checked her platinum blonde permanent wave in the mirror and Patrick took the revolver from under his seat. Got out the car into the humid early morning and checked the Cadillac's license plate. Was registered in Eumenides County.

Walked together into the diner and the sound of fans and smell of a greasy grill top and burnt coffee, a prematurely aged woman behind the fly-specked bar. Patrick and MaryAnn took a booth and was one of the two occupied.

Crowd at the other booth was men in sleeveless shirts showing sunburnt beefy arms sitting around a pussel-gutted man in shirtsleeves who was drinking coffee and holding court. Spoke in a deep bass drawl that sounded like confidence. Was telling his cronies about screwing a girl the night before.

"Think that's the man provided us our new Cadillac," Patrick said.

"He ain't bad looking for a local," MaryAnn said. She added "for a fat redneck," after Patrick gave her the eye and then gave the man in the booth with the Cadillac the eye, too.

Had brunette hair slicked to his forehead and a short beard the same brown as his eyes. Eyes were kind and sharp. Patrick caught those eyes looking over at him and the man sitting didn't look away and Patrick turned his head.

Had a big Colt .45 on his hip when he stood.

Came over to them before the waitress did. Wore boots that sounded like taps on the tile. In front of them, was only a hair older than Patrick. Just on either side of thirty.

"Saw y'all admiring my Cadillac," he said.

"It's a nice car," Patrick said.

"Sure is, boy. Bought it the same time I got fat," he said, holding his stomach and emphasizing his roundness.

"When was that?" Patrick asked.

"After I got rich."

"How you manage that?" MaryAnn asked. "Patrick and me tried our best and never was able."

"By being a mean bastard willing to do honest work," man said. "How folks got to calling me Hoss. I worked like one."

"Built like one, too," MaryAnn said. "Bet you built like one all over."

"Sure am," Hoss said. "But, darling, I got to ask myself if you old enough."

"Hoss, I surely am," MaryAnn said.

"Might need to see some identification, to satisfy myself." Scratched himself at the crotch. Had a prominent bulge in his jeans. Always had a hand on his gun.

"Happy to provide you some satisfaction," MaryAnn said. Got her purse and took out her ID. Handed it to Hoss who took it with the hand he'd used to scratch himself. Held it between two fingers and low so that he was still looking at them as he read it. Read MaryAnn's age out loud and then her full name, and then her listed address.

"What's a Southern girl doing with a Chicago address?" Hoss said.

"It's Patrick's place," MaryAnn said. Sounded oblivious to the implication.

"Goes with the license plate," Hoss said. "Boy," he added, "you got a license to be driving that car?"

"Sure I do," Patrick said.

"Registration, too?" Had an expression on his face like a man talking about his newborn child, smile showing teeth and drawing his cheeks in sharp lines. Patrick realized the boys at the other booth hadn't been talking since Hoss left them.

"Why you hassling us?" Patrick asked.

"Because I'm a mean bastard and you deserve it," Hoss said. "Boy drives into my county in a stolen car and first thing he does is decide to steal my Cadillac."

Put MaryAnn's ID in his pocket and MaryAnn wasn't flirting anymore. Her face was blanched paler than lead-white makeup and Patrick was sliding his hand toward the back of his pants. Sitting with his gun propped against the seat. Hoss was sunburnt and healthy-looking and cruel.

"Probably thought it would impress this one," Hoss continued. "Wonder what else you done to impress her."

"Nothing that concerns you," Patrick said.

"Now, boy, how I look at it, boy done so much wrong as you have come into my county, he becomes something that concerns me. Matter of justice."

"Why you think he's done anything wrong?" MaryAnn said.

"Because I can see wrongness on people clear as you can see I got brown eyes. Can feel it in my balls and my blood like I'm horned up."

Scratched himself again and hadn't lost his enthusiasm. Had never cared about laying MaryAnn.

"I think you're some sadistic local hick," Patrick said. Had his hand on his own gun now. "Who thinks being the big man in a hick redneck county makes him something."

"Well, boy," Hoss said, "my experience suggests that it does."

"Chicago would eat you alive."

"Ain't trying to be Al Capone," Hoss said. "Don't got to be, and I prefer not having the IRS and the G-men riding my ass."

"There's still the local law," Patrick said.

"Sheriff's my cousin and I fund his election campaign."

Felt the battered pistol grip. Shooting the sheriff's cousin was a quick trip to the gas chamber.

"MaryAnn," Patrick said, "let's get our breakfast someplace else."

Didn't have gas but could hitch a ride after abandoning the car. Steal another one from the son of a bitch stupid enough to give them a ride.

MaryAnn said she was following him. Didn't ask about getting her ID back. Hoss didn't move and didn't change his expression. Hadn't moved his hand from his gun.

"Y'all ain't leaving," Hoss said.

"We could drive away," Patrick said.

"Supposing I let you leave," Hoss said, "and you drive away in the same car you drove up in. I'd be obligated to call my cousin using the phone behind the counter. Read your girl's information back to him and tell him your license plate."

Boys at the booth were laughing now.

"My blood's telling me y'all won't make the county line."

Boys were laughing louder now. Patrick heard them like echoes in a vast empty space.

"I ain't never done anything wrong," MaryAnn said. "All I've done is what Patrick's done and taken me along for the ride."

"Bonnie got dead same as Clyde," Hoss said.

"You aren't going to just shoot us," Patrick said. "There's a law."

"You outside the law and come into my county," Hoss said. "Means you ain't got the law protecting you and all you've got is judgment waiting for you."

Hand was still by his gun and Patrick was eyeing the gun. Patrick had his, which he had taken off a dead Negro in Chicago. Shoot this fat redneck and run. Wasn't giving him a peaceful option. Shoot the boys at the booth, too, and the waitress behind the bar watching them for good measure. Leave no witnesses and drive out of Eumenides County in a dead man's Cadillac.

"I ain't dying here," MaryAnn said. "Patrick," she started shouting, "I ain't dying here!"

"Think your woman's telling you to use the gun you been fondling," Hoss said. "My blood's telling me you going to draw, boy."

Patrick pulled and raised the revolver to the table before Hoss put one in the side of Patrick's head. Dropped the revolver back on the table and Patrick's body dropped into the booth so he could look at the underside of the table. MaryAnn was screaming and the boys at the booth were making excitable noises like a tribal chorus.

"Blood don't lie," Hoss said. Sounded old and satisfied. "Bury you in my county, where you made your grave."

Told his cousin over the phone behind the counter that the woman had grabbed for the revolver, and that's why he'd shot her too. His boys agreed and the waitress said that she'd been in the kitchen. Sheriff got Patrick and MaryAnn's arrest warrants from Chicago before he drove to the diner to congratulate Hoss for doing good work.

# CONFEDERATE JASMINE

My wife poured tea from a tarnished kettle into a chipped chinaware cup with my family crest reproduced on its side. The cup rested on a saucer with a matching crest. The crest was what remained of my family inheritance. These worn pieces had been ordered by my wife from a Canton merchant by way of a British trading firm, the originals having been lost during the late war. But the crest remained to me, self-created by an ambitious and arriviste grandfather who believed that Mississippi needed an aristocracy to match Virginia and both branches of the same class of planters had been stripped of everything but their pretenses by defeat and Yankee troops.

My wife attempted a smile for our guest who had come to her Italian villa with the water stains in the corners of the grand salon and its mirrors with fine cracks and flaking gilt frames. Our guest was a man who had come to save us from the ruination to which we were much accustomed, or at least to stave off our final reckoning with poverty for some niggling period. Her resultant smile was as effective as could be managed by a woman who believed herself above serving others, even the prospective savior of her finances, and she was interiorly livid at not possessing the present means to import an English or French serving maid. The local Italian stock were cheap enough even for us, but it was wise not to overtax their capacity and I had advised it would be better received if she herself served, such a gesture appealing to a Yankee sense of magnanimous egalitarianism.

My wife with her title and so many pounds a year was an aristocrat as the term was understood in the United Kingdom, though the pounds a year had been dissipated before the celebration of my country's first declaration of independence, that which had occurred in 1776, and this was not the first time that I had exhausted her funds with so much of the year remaining hungry and tattered in front of us. My country's second and abortive independence was what had sent me on my European exile. While her country did not come to the aid of mine, she in person found the connection attractive.

My marriage was from a financial perspective favorable, as my wife has an income and capital I have drawn down. And to her resources I bring little of my own, for the Constitution of the nation of my citizenship forbids me payment for my wartime service and the pension to which a soldier of the winning side might expect, or payment for the manumission of my physical capital. I am left as ornamental as the paintings on the walls, and the creeping jasmine. An accent to her romantic High Toryism. She thought that she had found a Byron in me, or a Bonnie Prince Charlie with a drawl substituted for a brogue.

I have refashioned myself to suit her fancy. I appear in dress and manner more like a Cavalier than I ever had in Virginia. I have taken to wearing my hair long and powdered like a Jacobitic claimant to the throne of my wife's country.

I have made myself a sideshow Johnny Reb.

Through the French windows, open to the high summer and combating the villa's tendency toward draftiness, there was a wall of aged and red brick, trellised and laced with vines of Confederate jasmine in opportune bloom. The sweet, honeyed smell of the small white star-shaped blooms carried through the French windows to greet our Yankee visitor.

It was a delicate smell and powerful despite the delicacy. The scent caught on the air and was striking, though liable to dissipate on the passing breeze, and the blooms themselves lasted such a short time. Already, they were beginning to fall and littered the courtyard beneath the trellis with petals arrayed like supplicants at the sole remaining wall of a destroyed temple. I have never been to the Holy Places, though I suspect the sight of transient and mortal Jews at their immemorial Wailing Wall to be a macrocosm of what I have managed in miniature with my jasmine vines. The blossoms on the ground like supplicants and those white along the trellis like the papers stuffed into the crannies of the Wall as a means of prayer to the God of the Jews.

Our guest was a gentleman of the winning side. His suit was of a recent cut and the fabric had the sheen of newness, sharper for the threadbare and thinning fabrics of his hosts. My wife hoped that he might purchase some of the paintings on the walls, and perhaps some of the antique furnishings as well, perhaps the secretary desk or the Louis Quinze bookcase. She would offer to sell the books from the shelves, but those had already been sold to an antiquarian dealer to cover my debts to the Casino de Monte-Carlo accrued from baccarat.

Once we have sold all the pictures from the walls and the furnishings until the rooms are bare and peeling paper, should I continue gambling, which given my joyless proclivity for games of chance is near certain assuming my continued animacy, I will face the necessity of lowering myself to a profession. That terrible moment could be delayed should the wallpaper have some value to the appropriate merchant, and the frescos of reasonable antiquity cut from their place and transported, but that day of having to confront an occupation is as inevitable as surrender.

I idly wonder if my wife shall leave me before I exhaust the capital of her fortune. She would be justified, and I would bear little more than a minimum of resentment.

There are times I fear I have become generally inured to hardship, and to pleasure alongside it. I am left to a certain overarching dullness, an exiled sensation as though refuged from my own person. As though my actions are refracted through glass, a spectacle observed with subtle disfigurement.

My wife attempted pleasantries with our guest that day while I maintained a deliberately cold demeanor toward him. He wore what hair was left to him in an oiled part and counterbalanced with a fashionable heavy mustache and beard at the bottom. He had blue eyes of a sheen that matched mine, though heavier lidded and perhaps marked with fewer traces of excess and intemperance, though much of what he gained from Puritan teetotalism he lost from the overwork and exhaustion of Yankee enterprise. To such an extent upon our physiognomy, the effects of our relative inclinations toward work and dissipation counterbalanced us.

"I am lately of Arkansas," he said to my wife's polite inquiry regarding his state of residence, and rarely before the war had a resident of Arkansas announced his citizenship of that state with an accent familiar to the Boston Common.

"Little Rock by way of Salem," I said.

"I am a resident of Little Rock," he said. "Are you familiar with the state?"

"I never had the pleasure of knowing Arkansas."

"It is not so much of a pleasure, for the climate is unhealthful and malarial."

"What took you to Arkansas, then?"

"I entered the lumber business after the war. Arkansas is a fine state for virgin timber."

My wife poured tea for me, an occurrence heretofore unknown in the history of our marriage, and while facing toward me and away from our guest gave me the sort of look which might freeze the heart of a romantic heroine of faint constitution. I took her countenance to express that I was to comport myself around our prospective buyer, a purpose which my wife had attempted to impart verbally for no short time prior to his arrival.

"You made your fortune in Southern timber?" I asked.

"I have done respectably well for myself in my little section of our country. Though there are men who have made greater fortunes in the cities, and in the cattle trade, and most of all in the railroads. But, I have such as allows my daughters to study in Paris and myself to take the occasional collecting trip to the Continent."

"What do your daughters study?" my wife asked to prevent a harsher question from myself. Perhaps an inquiry into whether his residence could rightfully be described as his section, or whether it was truly our shared country.

Our guest brightened at her question. The Yankee affectation of the education of women so that they might be sharpers and tinkerers themselves, the crass pragmatism which was descended from the Puritanical valorization of labor for its own sake. Feminine education was rare beyond the decorative and household arts in the Southland, for my nation had recognized the superiority of the domestic style with its gentility.

"They study painting and the fine arts under tutors. According to their correspondence, they nurse ambitions of exhibiting at the Salon of the Parisian Académie."

This Yankee had carpetbagged to Arkansas to extract such wealth as could be stolen from the surrendered Confederacy, I thought. He had been only so modestly successful from his efforts as to afford an irregular and paltry imitation Grand Tour while his daughters learned decadence from a city which would have made Sodom blush with modesty. The effort at indignation was hard fought and in competition with a humorous sense of the grotesque meagerness of his gains as against my nation's losses.

"Do you have any sons?" my wife asked.

"My only son was killed in the late conflict."

It was a glad moment for me, or such as passes for gladness to me, for I was born one of four boys and was the sole survivor come the Surrender. I am not much given to forgiveness.

"Did you fight in it yourself?" I asked.

"I was a colonel on General William Tecumseh Sherman's staff."

"As I fear I would not have known him by his surname alone," I said, "I thank you for supplying the given name of the man who burnt a line through the Confederacy. But, may I ask, do you presently possess any railroad stock yourself, or do you only rip rail out of the ground rather than lay it?"

"I own some shares in a local venture," he said with a bothersome unflappability, "though not enough so that I may retire from the lumber trade."

My wife asked for my forgiveness and stated that perhaps my accent gave tell that I had fought on the opposite side.

"I gathered that," our guest said, "even by the strange manner of his dress."

"There are those of us who have not forgotten our country."

Our guest allowed himself a Puritan smile and a sip of his cooling tea.

"I have taken to drawing my blinds in Little Rock," he said. "There are men who did not accept the surrender and would take great pleasure in the assassination of a resident retired Yankee officer."

"I count myself one of those men who did not surrender."

"Though you have absented yourself from your country, rather than try to shoot a Yankee upstart in his home."

There were those of my countrymen who chose exile to Mexico, and some of whom served under the banner of Maximilian I. Pacific settlers or mercenaries, they had been variously scattered after the downfall of the emperor at Queretaro. Others had gone to Brazil, comforted by that more established empire's retention of chattel slavery and doomed to eventual incorporation. Their descendants would be eventually rendered indistinguishable from the surrounding half-Africanized, half-Europeanized society of that miscegenetic Latin nation.

I have chosen lonely exile and personal extinction. My wife was a woman of advanced years, not such as might attract attention and undue comment, but her barrenness was not such a surprise to me as it appeared to her. There is no successor to my country, but for its reincorporation and extinction, and I shall not have a successor to myself. There is nothing to inherit beyond a crest of recent creation. I shall not continue what has no future to it. That remains true to what principles remain to me.

"Some of us chose a quieter means of continuing our rebellion."

"So quiet as to be soundless," our guest said, "and what did you do during the louder period of your rebellion?"

My wife began on my behalf. Perhaps she feared that I would alienate our guest by claiming that I had spent the war drawing and quartering Yankee troops and restive Negroes. Her persuasive reasoning was intermingled with her habit born from the beginning of our relations to embellish my war record. For my wife was generally taken with the idea of marrying a great war hero, or at least a man with some gallantry to his person.

I had not yet touched my tea. Our guest finished his and listened to my wife with a supercilious mien. She narrated a history of the war in which I was a guiding personality of the conflict.

I became aware that I was possessed of a great tightness in my nerves, as though I were coiled into a ball and great force was contained within the coils. That, were I so armed,

I would jeopardize what security was known to my wife and myself by discharging a shot into our guest's bowels at short range. Though such an act would violate the basic rule of law against murder generally and the ancient moral prohibitions against the murder of guests specifically, I could justify such an action. I was possessed by a desire for revenge against this man who in his well-cut suit and prosperity represented a perfidious Yankeedom not content merely with the destruction of my home country, but driven by necessity to export itself abroad. Capital requiring export, and Yankeedom with its grand sense of liberatory mission likewise needing to expand itself to Arkansas and Italy. And, alongside this necessary export, a perhaps hypocritical simultaneous purchase of those objects of worth which could be brought into its insatiate maw.

Here then was a man of capital who had aggrandized himself on the corpse of my nation, and I would lower myself again to accept his payment made from my stolen national patrimony so that we might disburden ourselves of my wife's inheritance and a portion of our debts.

On the air, I caught the scent of my jasmine vines, their honeysuckle smell powerful upon a draft.

Confederate jasmine established, though artificially and transiently, in Europe. Petals falling and concurrent with their decline rendering alien air familiar to an exile.

I realized myself a Confederate abroad, and that I carry such remnant of my nation with me as might be maintained. Though my nation with its Temple formed of the Army of Northern Virginia was destroyed and I myself am unlikely to return from my captivity in this Continental Babylon, it is left to me to remember my country. Perhaps that is what is left to exiles, a kind of partial and occluded witness, fading with age and eventually vanishing into the grave.

Our guest was a bearer of more than witness, for he remained agent of his striving national will. Here was the dissolution of the Old South and the Old World. What they took from the South with arms they take from the Old World with dollars, and both accomplished by means of mass production and the factory system.

"Please forgive my wife her invention," I said. "In her telling, I have been a blockade runner, a cavalry commander, and aide-de-camp to General Lee himself."

"What were you in fact?" our guest asked, showing attention that had been wanting in conversation with my wife.

The scent would dissipate on the air, and my country disestablished, and I had become dissolute. There was little left to me with my affected cavalier dress and gambling debts except for honesty.

"Does it matter?" I asked.

"It is a question of fact."

"I find that romantic fancy is more favorable to my way of being."

"I am not a man of a romantic inclination. I might ask that I be humored with the unadorned facts."

"The unadorned facts," I said, "are superfluous. I am reduced to a mythology, a representative of a country that never existed."

"You had your three and a half years," our guest said. His tone was quizzical, as though he was currently unable to comprehend me but was confident in his ability to grasp my position and master it with a presently indeterminate but practicable number of questions.

"And the nearly three centuries from the founding of the Southland at Roanoke," I said. "Even before our independence was aborted, the country was not as it claimed to be, for it was meager and grasping and desperate in its way. Gentility was an ideal only shallowly attained, and our battlefield glories were short lived when our rival nations came to a contest. So, to live as a Confederate required living as a fiction, even before our defeat, and so perhaps my dress is more fitting than I had hitherto believed."

I was not ordinarily given to such comment. I ran a hand across my beard and through the carefully maintained curls of my hair resting over my collar.

Our guest motioned for another cup of tea. My wife, who had been listening to my disquisition with obvious horror and which horror remained even during my reflection, required me now to break my silence by verbally directing her to refill our guest's cup. She obliged. The tea had become cold in its kettle, but this development did not seem to concern our guest or my wife.

I considered, as this small ritual which was alien to her nature was enacted, the fate of our two persons. She an aristocrat born to a fortune secured by the Bank of England and fallen through marriage. I was a planter's son with aristocratic pretensions secured by chattel slaves and cotton acreage fallen through war and emancipation. Her family had made its fortune in shipping, bringing Negroes to my ancestral shore and cotton away from it, and though they had turned against the slave trade along with the Empire, it was perhaps fitting that she be reduced by wedding a descendent of the other great beneficiaries of that trade.

Jasmine came into the room in drafts. Another shipment overseas. Our guest sipped his tea and in so doing raised the crest my grandfather had chosen to his lips.

"My nation was built on half-willful delusion," I said, "from our aristocratic pretensions to our potential independence. To that extent, there was no Confederacy. Only a fever dream, born in the malarial tidewater."

"A fever dream that found itself well-established," our guest said.

"Our dream was carried as far west of the Mississippi as Texas, though it nestled itself most comfortably and paranoically in the deepest parts of the Southland. South Carolina which might have been Barbados transplanted to the mainland of North America. And Mississippi that produced Jefferson Davis. The state of my birth, by and by."

"And your dream took arms sufficient to rob me of my son."

He spoke without passion and as though from a great distance.

I managed some element of sympathy for this man. It was the first connection I had felt to a Yankee since Fort Sumpter, barring the connection engendered by hatred and bloodletting.

"He was killed in our death spasms, our convulsive twitching that culminated in Pickett's Charge."

"He fell after Gettysburg," he said.

"Then he died by our fatalistic automatism, not that the matter of the psychology of the army he faced mattered overmuch to him in his own dying."

"No," our guest said, "I suppose that did not matter to him. Dying by a beaten enemy is still dying, and clawing in the mud is the same in a winning cause as a defeated one."

"There is the difference of the commemoration," I said, "and the memorialization. There is a valor granted the victorious dead that is remembered as vain or pitiable regarding the defeated."

"That is departing far from relevancy, for the dying was the same. Remembrance does not affect the dead."

"But remembrance does affect the living, for we live in the mythology of a remembered and fictionalized past."

My wife attempted to interject, hoping likely enough to guide the conversation toward the visit's original purpose, the purchase of such articles of her personality as could secure ourselves against a hungry year.

Our guest spoke over her, and his voice was the stronger.

"Fiction," he said to me. "Fiction enough that you could imagine your war was won?"

I shook my head because such a denial would render my position as apparently deranged as an Indian fakir claiming that because all apparent events were illusory, the Sepoy Mutiny had never occurred. To that fakir, the Black Hole of Calcutta was reduced to a kind of figment of misguided sense impressions, a position perhaps difficult to convey to those suffering from an acute lack of breathable air.

Our guest understood the weakness of my position, and much as Grant had never withdrawn from Vicksburg though his initial sieges failed for the knowledge that with sufficient time and continued application of force, success would be inevitable, our guest pressed his advantage.

"Is this living in mythology?" he said and punctuated his speech with gestures taking in the room and its decay, for short of the smell of jasmine the room was in a wretched condition and obvious decline. "Can you deny your present squalor? Is it so easy to deny your obvious poverty?"

My wife began to speak, to defend the condition of her home. Our guest directed toward her such an expression of contempt as to render her silent. It had become a conversation between our guest and myself, and I had abandoned any notion that this visit would result in sale. Perhaps I should gain in self-understanding what I would forgo in compensation. Although such a gain would be of scant comfort to my wife who could not order an Italian serving girl to burn such understanding to heat a fire, and should hunger begin to press me later in the year I might then reconsider the reasonableness of my decision.

"It is perhaps living in the past, just as all of this company were drawn to Italy by High Renaissance memories, dimly remembered in these walls, rather than by the shabby nation that has been so recently reformed on the same soil which once nursed genius," I said.

"I believe you romanticize poverty, and perhaps such a position is easier than exalting the pursuit of wealth. Such an enterprise, divorced from what you could obtain by the driving of Negro slaves, was never much to your culture."

"The Southland was not a nation given to growth, that is true," I said. "And our planters were not so striving as the Yankee industrialists, seeking new unexhausted soils to grow our staples rather than new markets and new techniques, new organizational complexes to expand our fortunes. We were not a corporate society."

"Which defines those states which remained loyal to the Union?"

"Certainly," I said.

Though some Jews did return to rebuild their Temple, perhaps the greater share did not, and I know myself of my contemporary luckless majority. And should the Southland ever rebuild, in that rebuilding it would discover in itself a hitherto foreign dynamism for that is carried with growth like the multiplying tumors of cancer. In that growth the Southland would consume itself and dissolve in itself and become other to itself, and should it not perish entirely it would be as though a foreign land had grown like alien tissue on top of itself.

"And I imagine," said our guest, "that you view my own and my nation's faith in self-improving effort as a moral failing."

"I believe that you brought about the end of my world through such efforts. Do you believe a man, short of the most grotesque sort of scallywag, could find himself in wholehearted sympathy for such a mode of living?"

"I believe," our guest said, "that you have lost one fortune in a war of aggression and squandered another in idleness."

"I do not dispute either claim," I said, and in so saying knew I would not defend either my nation or myself. Both were unreformable and doomed. But we live and decline in accordance with our nature, and I will not deny that truth nor will I dress it in sentimental gloss.

"However, you have not placed yourself beyond criticism," I added.

"Then you do view my national character as a moral failing?"

"Not that, as much as the expansiveness of your aims. Your belief that you shall dissolve all things in your wealth and industry, and your denial of the dissolution of yourself. The dissolution of the blood."

I did not know the expression until I had uttered it, and I knew then that it encompassed the great shedding of blood that I had witnessed and the eventual stilling of the blood within my veins.

"That dissolution is the inevitable death of the self and the passing of all things," I continued. "The Southland is gone along with her cavaliers, and you who still half-unconsciously believe yourselves the Puritan elect of God shall pass as well."

"I have paid," our guest said. "My nation paid for being on the winning side, for you exacted greater casualties than we managed from you even in your defeat. And though I am of the winning side, I have paid my share of the bloodletting. There is no name to succeed me. I, too, shall, by your strange phrase, suffer dissolution."

"But you have breathed life into your corporate self, that shall survive you by inheritance through your daughters and eventual sons-in-law. For that corporate survival is a denial of the dissolution of the blood by means of wealth."

"A man might hope to have some survival beyond himself, however attenuated beyond his natural life. Children are one such way, and a corporate person another."

It was inevitable that a Yankee would believe he might survive by wealth. The South had attempted to perpetuate its breeding by devouring land and chattel. The Union attempted to perpetuate its wealth by accumulating capital and expanding its markets. In their contest, the latter had prevailed over the former. But capital was not so kind as breeding, and not given to a settled manner of existence.

Going to war without industry, believing ourselves knights and modern Cavaliers, we took no notice that the original Cavaliers had lost their conflict against the model Puritans.

We were living in our imagined past and extending it to the present. Sherman had recognized that war, stripped of its mythology, was a contest of industry. Industry, which was in contest with itself, competing against itself and destroying itself, consuming itself. The intermixed commercial and manufacturing processes which sent out representatives to collect more material to feed the grand infernal machine.

Capital that will not save its children and temporary stewards either, only swallow them and regurgitate them as new placeholders, new managers and owners and corporate identities, imagining themselves the masters of capital and failing to understand that the true master of capital is avaricious flux.

"Such an effort is to deny the dissolutive power of wealth," I continued. "Of devouring capital that swallowed my nation by surrounding it with iron rails and ironclad ships, by stamping rifles and ammunition and tinned foods. We are both men who shall be consumed. Myself by my past, and you by your future."

On the air, I smelt my jasmine blossoms. The small white stars bloomed along the worn brickwork, before me as though I were sitting at their base, supplicating myself. Here was something humane, and lovely, and delicate.

# DEATH POEM

After his first escape attempt, Lieutenant A.L. Forrest was locked in a tiger cage. His helicopter had been shot down in South Vietnam, and he had been humped along the Ho Chi Minh Trail into Laos. The Vietcong had carried him in a stretcher because he had broken his back. The rest of his men were dead in the crash and the firefight. They remained in the jungle, beneath the broken canopy.

When the helicopter had started to spin out, Private Reed asked him, "L.T., we're going to die, ain't we?"

Lieutenant Forrest had told Private Reed that they were already dead.

He had been tortured and had not signed the ready-typed confessions that were stained with his blood. He told the interrogator his name, rank, and serial number, and that he was already dead. Because of his captivity, he gained rank and lost several inches of height. He learned both after his eventual escape. The second escape, which was successful.

After the first attempt, was given time to recover so that he could be tortured again, and was able to escape with his fellow POWs. He had recruited them when they were handcuffed together and shackled with wooden blocks. All of them were eventually killed or recaptured.

Forrest, however, was rescued after signaling an American helicopter, flying illegally over the Laotian border. Forrest had spent days hallucinating from hunger and discussed the nature of suffering with Christ and the Buddha and Private Reed.

He was airlifted to Japan, and after he had gained enough weight was transported to the United States as a war hero. He wore his black Cavalry Stetson and saber when he received his medals. After an additional year of service spent in various hospitals, Captain Forrest received his honorable discharge and returned to Mississippi.

On the wall of his home, he pinned a picture of his crew next to crossed cavalry sabers he had inherited. His great-grandfather had worn sabers in the Confederate cavalry. His great-grandfather had raided Yankee rail depots, and the Yankee engineers had repaired the rail behind them. Captain Forrest had done search and destroy missions and the VC had returned as soon as the Americans left. His was a circular bravery, and futile, as his ancestor's had been.

He hung a South Vietnamese and a Confederate flag to go with the picture and sabers.

Captain Forrest sat by the Confederate jasmine vine that had motivated him to buy the home. Didn't leave except to buy beer and cash his VA checks.

Thought on the flags and his crew, and the crossed sabers. Smell of Confederate jasmine, and the smell would change and would be the overripe rotting jungle, and he would continue sitting where he was. Was the smell of death underlying the world.

After a time, he wrote a poem, and pinned it beneath the sabers:

*Vast hostile jungle.*
*A helicopter crashes through the canopy.*
*The sound of live rounds.*

After writing his poem, Captain Forrest stopped sitting by his jasmine vine. Didn't need to sit and think on the world and his war anymore.

# GLADIATOR MOVIES

"I could play Audie Murphy."

"You're too tall to play Audie Murphy."

"I ain't that tall."

"And even if you weren't too tall to play him, he's the kind of vain bastard who has got to play himself."

"Leaving aside whether that is vanity, I could play the kind of role Audie Murphy might play without being Audie Murphy or playing the role of Audie Murphy himself."

"What's wrong with the roles you're playing now?"

Duane Miller, who appeared under another name, which a Hollywood producer had picked out for him back when he was trying to make it in American pictures, was having an espresso with his friend Ross Goldsmith, also appearing in Italian films under a name he'd taken from Hollywood, at a coffeehouse that was popular with the Italian and expatriate American film set. Duane had fought the Martians on Mount Olympus across a soundstage in Rome that morning. He had been shirtless the whole time he was in front of the camera.

He had been in a kind of faux-leather half-tunic extending from the waist to his knees. This sartorial arrangement was marginally more dignified than the loincloth he'd worn when he was playing a knock-off Tarzan in his last jungle adventure picture.

"I ain't satisfied with my career," Duane said.

Duane was playing, well, in the Anglo-American release, he'd be playing Hercules, and in the Italian domestic version he'd be a gladiator character that only Italians had ever heard of, and in the French and the West German versions he didn't know and didn't much care. Dubbed him even in the English version, and the dialogue wasn't the draw any more than the plot. He was thankful for the censors because the Italians would have him stark naked in front of the camera like Jane going for a swim in *Tarzan and His Mate* if it meant the picture selling more tickets. He wouldn't have grounds to protest because he was already selling his body for a living.

"You ain't satisfied with being the lead in a feature and having another waiting for you after shooting on this one wraps," Ross said like he was asking a question that didn't need answering for being plainly ridiculous.

Duane had gone to UCLA on a wrestling scholarship and gotten into the Muscle Beach scene. Ross had been a UCLA football hero and "Hoss" to his friends because he'd always looked like one even before getting into the same scene. Was how they'd met and hearing each other's drawls had formed a quick friendship. They had been partners in an informal, handshake enterprise that had involved the pooling of their resources and paychecks for the last several years of their lives.

"Ain't even satisfied being borderline rich. Considering how we was when we got on that transatlantic flight from

Los Angeles to Rome, having spent everything we had between us on the tickets. And me having more to spend on this enterprise because I was always better at taking a fall doing stunt work. And after the tickets both of us having the clothes we had on and our passports and not much else."

"Sure, we was broke. Ain't denying that. But what's that got to do with me being unsatisfied now?"

"Boy, we weren't just broke, we was flat busted. And my point's that, considering where we is now, being dissatisfied is practically being ungrateful for the life we've made ourselves here."

They were both wearing hand-tailored Milanese suits with unusual measurements and pretending they liked Italian coffee. On first meeting, had both been in bathing suits and getting Coca-Colas out of an icebox.

"I ain't ungrateful for what we done," Duane said, "and you weren't no better at stunts than I was. Just had that director was a football nut and liked throwing you work."

Both of them had learned how to ride a horse and shoot guns early in life. Didn't take too long to master falling off a horse without getting hurt and throwing a fake punch that looked real, and that was enough for stunt work.

"Boy, that director liked throwing me work because I was a goddamned star stuntman. Could drop and transfer horses like Yakima Canutt and never missed a mark or made life hard for the second-unit man stuck filming the scenes the director didn't bother himself to shoot."

"There ain't no such goddamned thing as a star stuntman," Duane responded and was a familiar point from back when they were only stuntmen, "because being a star means folks on the street recognize you for being one and pretty girls want to lay you for being up on that big screen. And in the history of stuntmanning it ain't never fucking happened that a pretty girl gone up to a stuntman and said I thought you was so impressive doing the stunt the lead is too chickenshit and expensive to do himself that I'd like to get down on my knees and learn you something."

The transition to acting not involving falling off a horse and with their faces in focus had been rockier than getting into stunts. Duane and Ross were both of a distinct physical type and possessed what a generous acting coach had described as a limited range. Ross liked to point out they were both better built than Marlon Brando and talked about how that ought to be enough because that was what folks were going to see, a man looking good with his shirt off and none of that Method bullshit. Method and acting schools was all a put-on, an excuse for folks to go see a real goddamned stud actor and tell themselves it was art.

That being Ross's position and reasonable on its face, Duane had wondered why Brando got better roles than they did in spite of them being better built than Brando was. And them not mumbling their lines purposefully.

"Boy, a star stuntman can get work doing stunts and ain't vain enough to complain that the camera ain't interested in his face," Ross said. "Knowing there won't be no face on the screen until the cut to the close-up of the lead looking pretty and not at all like he just fell under a horse."

"Sure, that's why there ain't no such thing as a star stuntman."

"Remember that crazy German director wanted me to jump that ravine on horseback?" Ross asked like he was ignoring a stupid comment to concentrate on the main point. "Easiest jump you ever made but qualified as life-endangering?"

"Sure I do," Duane said and he had known this story would come up. Had come up near enough to every day in their relationship since it had happened, and Duane still wasn't convinced it had actually happened to Ross and not some other lucky son of a bitch.

"I make that jump," Ross kept going like he hadn't heard, "and know that I'm now contractually entitled to my hazardous pay. But the director, little German fucker with a megaphone," Ross mimed a megaphone with his hands, "says to me, du n-EE-d to do de jump A-GAIN, for de light." Ross was making himself heard over the background noise at the coffeehouse, vowel-rich chatter and construction machinery building the postwar miracle. Ross was indifferent, seeing as the two resident stars weren't likely to get kicked out unless they started beating the shit out of somebody or each other. "So, what do I do, polite bastard that I am?"

"You jump the horse again."

"But what do I call back before I make the jump?"

Duane fiddled with the bothersome small cup of coffee that the Italians chose to serve. "You call across to the director," Duane said.

"Know that from the question, but what was it I said?"

"You called at the top of your voice, I get paid the same for every jump."

"And that crazy German had me jump that ravine ten times and I made more than a month of steady work that afternoon."

Duane hadn't never had that kind of luck. Never even thought to claim he'd had that kind of luck. Ross had put the money under the mattress, and he'd had to earn it somewhere.

"That right there is star stuntmanning, even if the girls don't give a shit."

Not so long after Ross had made plenty of money claiming he'd jumped a horse repeatedly across a ravine, Duane had started spending his share of his money on acting lessons. Ross had said that acting lessons were taught by folks couldn't make a living acting and consequently weren't worth shit and went about proving it by going out for parts himself. He started getting small parts playing the secondary heavy, the mean looking bastard who gets beat up at the end of the first act to show the lead actor is a serious man. Not so often he could stop stunting, and not so much they had any money between them after the cost of living, but he got on camera and had his own lines. Liked to announce he could do his own stunts, and damn if he didn't in every one of his speaking roles. Not that the audience gave a damn, but it got him a little reputation with casting. Once got thrown through a screen door had been rigged to fail, and instead went right through it, landed on his ass, and kept going with the scene and the take had made it into the final cut and it looked badass even if he did lose the fight.

Meanwhile, Duane kept at his lessons and started auditioning for substantial roles. Chasing the lead in B pictures and supporting roles in features. Ended up doing the stunt work without the something extra in his pay stub or having his name deep in the credits that Ross was getting. When they got on the plane to Italy, Duane hadn't said a word on camera over the course of his career, and Ross had. Since getting to Italy, Duane still hadn't.

"Even if that is being a star stuntman instead of getting lucky with a crazy director didn't give a shit about busting his budget, there's still no appreciation for it," Duane said.

"You mean girls ain't going to get naked for you because you ain't on a film poster?"

Duane shrugged because that was a kind of appreciation which they hadn't got while they were working stunts. Ross had gotten some of it after he started getting small roles, not as though name actresses were laying him even if he claimed he'd been to bed with some of them, but starlets who played chorus girls and waitresses who went to too many matinees had certainly shown him affection.

"But," Ross said, "that gets to the root of why you being uppity, because answer me this, if you was inclined, could you get near enough to any girl walking along the street from here to the studio?"

"Why near enough?" Duane asked.

Ross looked at him like he was tired of being the brighter member of the partnership.

"Because some girls is crazy and some girls is blind and some are faithful to their husbands and some ain't never been to a movie theater because they ain't got the time, and some girls only like other girls which you have to pay extra for but presents some complications at the pick-up stage, and all those potentialities together mean that aiming for one hundred percent is flat unrealistic."

Duane said that was fair enough because he had trouble arguing with the logic. Was occasionally reminded that Ross had actually finished college. Duane had enjoyed himself too much and found the California sunshine was good for his complexion and bad for his meager academic motivation.

"So," Ross continued, "subject to that condition, how you situated right now in Italian pictures, could you get laid by near enough to any girl walking down the street?"

"I suppose that's true," Duane said.

"You're damned right that's true, and that's the ingratitude. You got yourself a situation now where you got more money and more of it than you can handle. Boy, you used to live to show yourself off on the beach with hardly a stich on you, and now you acting like you above taking your shirt off to give the audience something they want to see."

What carried them in Europe was they were both studs. On a continent where nobody heard an actor's real voice and there wasn't enough money for prestige dramas except the tiny art pictures only Left Bank intellectuals pretended to watch, being a lead was as simple as having an American face and a body looked better than Brando's. Ross had initially pitched the idea of going to Europe and Duane had let himself be convinced. Ross could've gone on his own but had said they were going to get rich together or else they were going to stay poor in the pleasure of each other's company.

"There's still the critics," Duane said.

The coffeehouse had an autographed poster of them in a picture they'd done together, released in America under the title *Romulus & Remus Battle the Titans*. Duane was shirtless and posed so his muscles looked good and Ross was wearing cardboard armor and looking substantial. This was after they had both become names and were getting fees per picture which hurt their teeth, and they'd both been placed over the title even if Duane's name came first when reading from the left.

"Boy, that's the kind of statement show's you ain't living in reality. You want, what do you want, a good write-up in the dailies and an award?" Ross said.

"Would tell folks I'm really an actor."

Ross pointed at the poster using all of his hand and putting some shoulder into it.

"Boy, that right there's what tells folks you an actor. You got an audience and a payday and your name over the title. That's being an actor. In point of fact, because the poster's got you shirtless and posed like Charles Atlas, that is being a stud actor."

Duane was thinking that it was always his body. Had made it to college on his body. Had washed out of college because he'd enjoyed being good looking on the beach. Had stunted because his body could handle it. And now he was making his money on his body and if he'd been a whore that would've been the only thing he hadn't sold already.

"A body can want respectability, can't he?" Duane said. "After he's made some money for himself and a name, can't he need to have some respectability?" Ross's features arranged themselves heavily like a defensive lineman who was going to stop an unwise rush attempt. He was naturally redheaded, despite the rumors, and grew it long so that with the attention of a set hairdresser it would curl how gladiators in the pictures wore theirs. Otherwise, besides his arms being better defined and his fashion sense having improved when he was dressed, looked how he had before he went to college. Living on the beach and the Mediterranean hadn't managed to tan him.

"You ain't thinking about trying for Hollywood again?" Ross said.

Duane blushed through his tan because that was it exactly. Same as he had taken to bodybuilding more smoothly than Ross, had a coloring that suited tanning and a build that suited putting on aesthetic muscle. Ross had always been too heavy for the sport, which was why he was wearing that cardboard tunic on the autographed poster. In the big gladiatorial coliseum fight scene between them, handled using a matte print and some extras in bleachers, and sand across the soundstage floor, Ross had been wearing a kind of plastic chain-mail shirt and heavy mask. Looked real frightening, by genre standards, and before they'd learned they were brothers in that picture and reconciled he came close to walloping Duane. Duane managed to outfox him and threw sand in his mask so he could win the fight, what with being listed first and all. But Ross had been real intimidating and sold the whole scene just using his body, didn't dub his voice because he didn't have dialogue during the fight.

Duane was the first to admit that Ross could outlift him any day of the week, but the girls didn't seem to care so much and the queers didn't either, or the boys who were apparently heterosexual but came to these pictures anyway.

"Well, I got some money in the bank," Duane said, "and I got so that I got a name even if it ain't my own. My agent thinks he could line me up a real role."

Didn't want to admit to knowing that Ross was also the better actor, even if it was a marginal advantage in their current circumstances. Duane was commanding higher fees and their next picture together wouldn't be any question that he'd be listed first. His career was on the steeper rise, and it was because he had the better body and the better tan and the better hair, and he was going to use that rise to make something more out of his career than just being the body that looked better stripped nearly nude.

"Boy," Ross said, "what we doing here are real roles. For boys like us, these are the prime goddamned roles of our lives. Back in America there's just a few years of stunting followed by some long years working construction when the money runs out. You ain't going to like laying tar on a summer day."

"Ain't going to end up working construction. I got money in the bank."

"You got the money to retire?"

Duane didn't answer. Them living out of a common pot rendered the question rhetorical.

"Then you ain't got the money such that you ain't taking a bad risk," Ross said. "You'd be sacrificing years of roles for a shot at playing Tarzan and your agent is a goddamn liar if he's saying that is a sure thing. And even if you do land Tarzan you going to be playing Tarzan and that ain't hardly more respectable than what you playing now."

"But, here," Duane stumbled for words same as he had when he was reading his lines auditioning in Hollywood, "goddammit, they dub our voices. Ain't even really me, without my voice. All I am here's a moving picture with his shirt off."

"And I'm a boy who looks real mean with his shirt on. Worse rocks to build a career on."

On set that morning, Ross had lifted a foam boulder off of his co-star using his back like Atlas. Duane thought that had put the metaphor into his head. Co-star was a Spanish girl with jet dark hair and matching eyes who was laying him for her career. She had enough English to tell him she'd grown up in a brothel which used to be a convent, and that she thought her father was an American. Ross had bragged to Duane that he had told her that his daddy was an American too and patted her on the ass and laid her to satisfy his desire to screw a dark-haired Spanish girl who thought it was clever to say she was half-American.

Looking mean and leveraging it had been real rewarding for Ross.

"But, I mean, you ain't never had, you ain't never had the sort of ambition, the kind of artistic ambition like I'm talking about," Duane went on.

"Boy," and for the first time Ross said boy like it might be a threat, "don't mix up being smart with being unambitious. I been bringing more money into this partnership until just about yesterday, and I was the one set us up in Italian films to begin with. Why we ain't still stuffing our faces at every cast and crew buffet since we didn't have the money to waste on a hamburger and fries for ourselves is because I was the smart bastard who said there was money in Europe being muscled-up and stripped."

"There's wanting to be more than muscles, and I'm the one who gets told to strip," Duane was getting his own edge. "Because I'm the one looked like Steve Reeves out on the beach and try as you would you never could stop looking like a defensive lineman. Only roles you could get in Hollywood in front of the camera was the heavy because there ain't no lead actress would touch you if she didn't think it would help her career."

"Sure," Ross said, "I look like what I am, and I ain't a dumbass pretending I'm something other than what I am."

"Yeah, you sure are authentic. You're an actor making a living playing a role gets translated three or four different ways and appearing under a name that sounds better than the one you was born with."

"And you chasing authenticity even if it's going to wreck you. And you still going to be doing it with a name ain't yours."

Their suits were both straining. Puffing themselves out against the unusual measurements.

"My great granddaddy raided with Nathan Bedford Forrest," Duane said. "That fucker sharpened his saber to the hilt. And what do I do? I wave a piece of plastic around with my shirt off. I ain't even an actor. I'm just a bitch-boy gets on a soundstage and flexes. No different than a stripper teasing down to a G-string."

"You ain't a bitch-boy," Ross said, "you're a fucking stud actor, same as I am. I watched plenty of bitches strip and it ain't what you doing."

"You just afraid that me being a bitch-boy means you the same because we in the same goddamn business."

"I ain't a goddamn bitch-boy and neither are you," Ross shouted and was enough to be heard across Laurel Canyon.

By this time the coffeehouse had recentered its attention on the two very large and well-known American actors shouting at each other in regional accents too thick for the bystanders to follow. A local who supplemented his income as a paparazzo had his camera on his table and was poised to capture what he was sure to be an oncoming brawl over a woman, because what else could those two massive and clearly oversexed Americans be arguing about? They kept shouting a term for women and a term for sex the paparazzo had learned while pimping to Americans during the occupation.

"We both just a step above pornography. I can't even send my momma photos of what I'm doing."

"This ain't porno," Ross said, "and I'm the one talked you out of stripping for those skin mags, threatened to beat you to death and send them to your momma if you did. And thank God because right now you'd be getting blackmailed out of your ass with those like Marilyn Monroe."

Duane felt his position was being undermined, and worse by a line of argument he had advanced without prompting.

"And, fuck," Ross continued, "didn't you buy your momma a house? And didn't you once tell me she don't even like going to the pictures?"

"That's true."

"Then what level of flying fuck can she possibly give about your career?"

Was like they deflated. The tension had gone out of them how it always did before they blew.

"That's true, too," Duane said, admitting defeat and changing the subject, "but, still, Jesus, it ain't stripping maybe, but it still ain't even my voice. It's my body and somebody else's voice dubbed over me same as for all the Dagos, in movies that ain't about Greece or Rome or science fiction or nothing like that. Just a weird muddle getting thrown together by a screenwriter and a director who don't give a shit between them. I'm mixed together in pictures that are all mixed together too, and there ain't a center there."

Ross, whose latest involved battling an undersea race of Atlanteans led by Neptune, a West German actor he'd worked with before whose professionalism he respected even if they couldn't carry on a conversation for lack of a shared language, shrugged and signaled to the paparazzo to show him Ross knew he was there and if he took a picture he'd catch a beating.

"Ain't going to argue that what we do's got much fidelity to the source material."

"But it ain't nothing at all. It ain't even so that a body can imagine it's real, all muddled together how it is," Duane said, "it ain't authentic to nothing."

"We get in front of a camera and run around and do what the director and the script tell us we ought to," Ross said, "nobody except Brando thinks that's got anything to do with reality."

"But," Duane said, "think about playing a Viking. Back when there was real Vikings, those boys got themselves worked up so they believed they was wolves and bears, and they went out and slit throats."

"Sure, they was badass and all that."

"That's right, but me, I know I ain't a Viking even when I was playing one."

"That was a good picture," Ross said, "made plenty of money."

"No, it weren't a good picture because it didn't make any goddamn sense. And all the time I was acting in it, I just had my eye on hitting my marks. And that's to my point, because even if I got it in me to be a naturalistic actor, there wouldn't really be a Viking even then. How they knew they were wolves and bears before they went out on a raid. That's authentic. Being somebody else, and not even knowing that you're somebody else. That somebody else is so total and complete that it's real even for being fake. Without that completeness, all we doing is playacting."

"Sure, what we doing is playacting, that's what I been saying. Well-compensated playacting."

"But," Duane said, "it's more than that. Even if I did a war picture, I ain't going to be a soldier. I'll be playing some sense of a soldier, pulled together from real soldiers and soldiers from other pictures and soldiers how writers imagine soldiers are. And it'll be a goddamn mess."

Ross rubbed his temple and was weighing whether he ought to throttle some sense into Duane. Wouldn't even be out of hostility, so much as a frustratedly earnest desire to set him right.

"You bitching about being an actor or about being an actor in something ain't any good?"

"I'm saying, not only ain't I Audie Murphy, and not only ain't I playing Audie Murphy, I ain't even playing in a war picture that ain't an embarrassment to the folks came before me who were actual soldiers."

Ross brightened up because here was a problem could get solved. "You want to do a war picture's got authenticity to it? We'll put our own money in it, do it ourselves. You'll play a man in gray and so will I. We'll hire somebody who's got talent to write the script and another somebody who knows what he's doing to direct. We'll end up co-owning the picture and when it's a hit we'll make a bundle."

"General Lee, how you never seen him before," Duane said, "buff and with his shirt off?"

"Boy," Ross said and was sounding excited, "you can play a soldier and take your shirt off in a love scene that'll convince the distributors that it's all marketable and everybody in the audience will understand why she's laying you."

"It'll be an Italian woman and all the other folks in it'll be Italians or French or Spanish playing white folks. Hell, playing Confederates, it's practically sacrilegious."

"Ain't like Vivian Leigh or Leslie Howard were from the Southland," Ross said.

"They weren't Southern?" Duane asked and looked like he'd been told there weren't any God in Heaven and it was just empty air above him.

"Hardly anybody was except the Negroes. Still went over bigger than life in Atlanta."

Ross's mood had improved along with his position in the conversation. Had substituted thrashing Duane in an argument for thrashing him physically and the effect was soothing. And he was willing to try and make some serious money together, and convince Duane to stay in Italy.

"Still, though," Duane said, "a woman can't nobody believe is from the South playing a Southern girl waiting for her soldier-boy to come home and when he gets back from Appomattox he's built like Hercules. Still going to be muddled."

"Ain't nothing to it except acting and dubbing the bitch's voice with a Southern accent. Nobody wants to watch a boy looks half-starved and raggedy get with his girl anyway, all the war heroes in pictures got some good health to them."

"That ain't right," Duane said. "Ought to need more than that. A picture needs some center to it."

Ross relaxed. "All there is to it's what the audience will accept. And us getting paid."

"You got yourself that woman," Duane said, "all that talking about me being ungrateful and I bet you want a girl's got more than a dubbed voice to her."

"Sure I do," Ross smiled self-satisfied, "a real sweet bitch who learned English in a brothel. Knew what everything meant and even learned me some words for some real pleasant activities. And she don't mind having her voice dubbed in the picture and don't mind our conversation being mostly about what we doing in bed."

"You a true romantic."

"We both know what we want and ain't above getting just what we want."

"Sounds like you being authentic," Duane said and felt clever.

"Everything I'm fucking doing is authentic, I just don't look down on what I am."

"And what are you?" Duane asked.

"I'm an actor, and a bodybuilder, and a piece of white trash managed to get an education and's now making some fucking money and getting laid and got my name on a poster. That's what I fucking am and I'm goddamned proud of myself and you ought to be, too."

"But," Duane started and looked a worser kind of deflated like he knew the future was aging and sagging, and decay and the collapse of the faddish market for their kind of films, "none of this matters. We ain't in movies that matter. They ain't some famous Greek tragedies that people remember, just some weird and twisted version of them. More than that, we ain't going to be actors when we die. We going to be remembered as bodybuilders who made some godawful movies. Ain't that depressing that we never really going to be better than Muscle Beach bums that went to Italy?"

Ross leaned back and threatened the chair. Breathed out and here was a problem because Duane wasn't wrong. They had fought the Olympians, the Titans, and the Atlanteans, in addition to some invaders from a couple of planets. They couldn't discriminate between them any more precisely than the audience, although they did remember which paycheck went with which picture.

Ross turned his head on a bull neck and looked at the poster of the two of them. That picture was the last time they had gotten equal billing.

"Matters," said Ross, "because we ain't got no choice but to live as actors. Because being bodybuilders was a step to becoming actors, was an expression of our having the need to show ourselves off."

"Saying this is all me being vain."

"That ain't quite what I'm saying," Ross said without defensiveness. "It's rather that we both got to be seen. That's simply how we are, don't even necessarily got to involve ego though I suppose it does involve some of that."

"Got to be strutting around on a soundstage more than half naked, because that's what I am? A boy needs folks to see too much of me?"

"I think that we all got to wear masks, and that you put on a mask by taking off your shirt."

Duane chuckled at that because it was a funny way of looking at what he was doing. Only the one of them who'd managed to get through college would have thought of it that way.

"I ain't kidding," Ross said. "You talking about authenticity and part of being authentic is the part you play being necessary to yourself."

"It's necessary that we do silly fucking movies that nobody could possibly give a damn about and ain't got nothing to them?"

Ross nodded like he was goddamned right. There was a path to their lives and he was seeing that path.

"It's every bit of it necessary," Ross said. "I was told once that there's a necessity to good and evil in this world. If that's so, then it stands to reason there must be some necessary idiocy to it as well, to balance out the seriousness. How those Greek tragedies always ended with a comedy. World needs something that ain't so serious, there's a necessity to that. And we're the performers needed for the part of it that ain't serious, how there's the Method actors to put out seriousness."

Duane rubbed his hands. He had calloused his palms from weightlifting.

"I suppose there's something to that," Duane said. "Only, we ain't doing the important kind of picture if there even is an important kind of picture."

"What I'm saying is that we are part of how the world makes sense of itself. We making sense of ourselves and the world making sense of itself. Whole world is an effort at understanding itself."

"Me fighting the Martians shirtless is the world making sense of itself, whatever that fucking means?"

"I ain't saying that it makes a whole lot of sense to us. Because, goddamn, it ain't something that is amenable to logic but there's a sense to it regardless. Only, trying to impose order on it would ruin the whole structure. Because there's got to be something senseless and chaotic how the dramatic is well-structured and ordered with every line of the script and every performance thought through and reasonable. We the folks doing the part which is throwing paint at the canvas and seeing what's there at the end."

"All there is at the end's a mess."

"Naw, that ain't true. There's chaos to it, but there can be something there worth seeing if you ride it right."

"They're pictures ain't nobody thinks are art," Duane said, "where a bodybuilder playing Samson in the American version whips the villain's ass and gets the girl and don't die in the temple."

"It's a picture and it's religion and it's entertainment. You got yourself over the marquee and you fight like Samson. Only instead of dying like Samson, you tear down the Temple of Baal and walk out unscathed and fuck the blonde girl that looks better than Delilah at the end."

"Doubt that captures the story."

"It's a different story, and the world's got a place in it for stories with a simpleminded happy ending."

Duane said that was sure fine and suggested they leave the coffeehouse because the paparazzo was impatient to get photos of them slugging at each other.

So they stepped out into the Roman street and was a poster for Duane's latest plastered on the wall across the narrow way. Had single-billing, and his Hollywood name was prominent above the title. The sun reminded Ross of Muscle Beach, and as they started walking toward the studio their walk took the stride they'd developed, confident and arrogant and proud, showing off way back on the Southern California coast.

Passed the girls and the cheap scooters and the expensive cars. They were better dressed than most, and Duane with his coloring might have passed and Ross but for his coloring could have passed for prosperous Italian businessmen enjoying the postwar boom. Were both remembering bumming along Muscle Beach. Those had been the days they'd learned what they'd been missing, growing up in Georgia, below the Fall Line.

Duane checked his imported watch and saw they'd been talking too long, and he was pushing being late for the next shoot.

"Why do you care so much about my career?" he asked.

"Jesus Christ, it ain't occurred to you that we the only friends the other's got in this world?"

They walked with mutual recognition.

"You remember me saying I needed some time before we came to Italy?" Duane asked.

"Sure I do," Ross said.

"You ever wonder why I needed that?"

"I figured you were antsy about hopping on a plane to Europe."

"There was that, but there was something else. I was waiting to hear about a role."

"Course you were," Ross said, "you were always waiting on a role."

"Was trying to play Samson in a Bible picture."

"Would have had to be that or Tarzan."

"And you know how I knew I had to come to Italy?"

"When you didn't get the role?" Ross said.

"I knew I had to come to Italy when I was told I was too muscular to play Samson. Producer told me I might be able to get the role if I slimmed down."

"Fuck that," Ross said.

"That's what I said to the producer. Fuck that, and I'm going to Italy. Least over there when I take my shirt off, they'll say I've got the fucking part as I am."

"And you ended up playing Samson anyway."

"Least in the American release," Duane said.

They were within sight of their studio. Duane would go and strip and fight the Martians, and Ross would go and strip a little less and fight the Atlanteans for less pay and lay his co-star after. And while Ross was laying that actress who wanted him for her career, Duane would sleep on whether he would tell his agent to get him that part playing Tarzan, and if he was going to make another run at a Hollywood career.

"Speaking of, in addition to being too tall, you're too muscular to play Audie Murphy," Ross said.

"What?"

"You ain't lean how real soldiers are. Ain't the right physical type. Might be you'd have to slim down for it. Otherwise, would be that same muddled thing you been complaining about, a bodybuilder playing a soldier who looks like a bodybuilder."

"Boy," Duane said, "you can go straight to hell."

"And come right back to Italy," Ross said, "better here than it was when Audie Murphy was fighting his way up it."

"That's true," Duane said looking straight ahead toward the studio like he was thinking about his future, "but Audie Murphy came back from hell and went straight to Hollywood. Didn't go back to Italy."

"Ain't the same Italy that it was," Ross said.

They passed a line of garish posters, some with their names that weren't really theirs and others with the professional names of other boys built like them. He was thinking about the war picture he and Duane were going to produce together, and their future as shared as their recent past. Could be they'd buy a business together. Either here or back in America and tell each other war stories from their acting days. Later in life, would maybe receive mail from an errant fan who happened to catch one of their pictures on television and saw some worth to it, even if the picture was only being aired as filler. They wouldn't be a name back home, how their European career was going. Were just two boys had disappeared somewhere on Muscle Beach. Turned into, well, whoever they were now, the names on the poster, or Duane and Ross talking with each other knowing the whole rest of the world thought of them as somebody else. But they were on that poster. That meant something. Being comfortable was something and being a face on a film poster was something. There weren't a lifetime's worth of gladiator movies. Audiences would go onto something else.

# Campus Radicals

Minnie had her purse and Artie, her husband, held onto the briefcase with the money. They were parked at a motel far outside the city limits to meet a man who sold guns. Minnie and Artie needed guns because they were revolutionaries. Their group, which called itself the American Red Army Faction and was composed of graduate students at the state university, had been forced to reevaluate its plan to arm itself after the workshop hadn't worked out. The workshop had been a bomb-making operation in Felix Greenbaum's basement which had detonated early. Had taken out Felix's townhouse and perforated his eardrums and so there wasn't a workshop anymore and Felix was out a townhouse and kept asking people to repeat what they had said to him. Self-sufficiency not being a viable option, they'd needed to find a supplier.

After the coordinating committee had decided that making an outreach to the Hells Angels was counterrevolutionary (because the Angels were fascists), and after the Black

Panthers told them to go fuck themselves, they found an independent Negro revolutionary who, after selling Minnie a snub-nosed pistol stolen out of a rich lady's purse, told them about Earl.

"You want some real heavy metal revolution fighting shit, you've got to go see Earl," he had said. "Earl's a man who lives to sell guns. Came up here from down South and started supplying firepower to all the folks that need it."

Minnie had unilaterally handed over the rest of their ready funds and had gotten an unlisted number and instructions. Minnie called that number and left a message saying she had to meet Earl and describing what kind of firepower she was looking to buy, and the next day she'd got a call back from a second number with a white woman's voice on the other end saying when and where she was supposed to meet Earl and how much cash she needed to bring.

That was when Minnie informed the central committee about their new supplier. Artie asked her to get the deal cleared in advance and started to talk about party discipline and democratic centralism and Minnie told him to shut up and that the central committee would go along with the plan because it was a good plan and they didn't have any other one.

"We aren't going to beat pig power and the fascist power structure using nonviolent means," Minnie said to Artie. Wasn't the first time she'd said that, seeing as it had been Minnie who'd initially decided their Marxist reading group was becoming a revolutionary cell and needed to procure weapons. She chose herself as General Secretary, how Brezhnev was for the Soviets, although the group's position on the revolutionary purity of the USSR was uncertain.

Minnie assured the committee that Earl wasn't part of the organized fascist element, and the central committee rubber-stamped the General Secretary's plan. The well-heeled WASPs had called their daddies in Kansas and Nebraska and the wire transfers came through how they always did. The Jews had contributed what they could from their TA pay and part-time jobs.

Artie had packed the money in the briefcase and held onto it while Minnie drove them out into cow country. The motel advertised nightly rates and color TV and jacuzzi bathtubs, and had a swimming pool that was the color of an algae bloom. She parked next to a beat-up truck, a declining cherry red.

"We couldn't meet him at a nice hotel in the city?" she asked.

"I guess we couldn't," Artie said.

"And not even at a decent hour."

"Maybe he's a morning person."

Earl had set their time at seven-thirty in the A.M.

"You have what we need?" Minnie asked, ignoring what Artie had said.

"I do."

"You have it where you can reach it?"

"I put the gun in the briefcase how you told me to."

"That's not what I said. I told you to put it where you could reach it if we need to defend ourselves. If he decides to kill both of us, you'd have to open the briefcase to get to the gun. Think how much time that'd take."

Artie knew Minnie had told him to put the pistol in the briefcase. She had emphasized the point repeatedly since she was the one who had decided they needed to be armed.

"I'll, well, Minnie, I don't have any other place to put it."

"God, I'll have to take care of it myself."

She got out of the car and Artie followed. She knocked and there was a pause and a shadow over the peephole and then the door opened.

There was a man. He was big and holding a suitcase full of something which a federal agency would most certainly confiscate and use as evidence in a court of law. This must have been Earl.

Earl had gray eyes and full brown hair that was slicked back, and a weightlifter's biceps and sharp chest over a bloated gut. He was wearing a tight sleeveless T-shirt that showed the tattoos along his arms. Had a cross in a plain Protestant design, an Imperial Eagle with SPQR beneath it, and a Viking that looked like a blond pulp barbarian with runes that might have meant something in Norse beneath that. T-shirt had a Confederate flag on it.

Artie feared that Earl wasn't their scene.

"Y'all my morning appointment?"

Earl scratched his belly with his free hand beneath the flag and looked them over. Artie knew what Earl saw. Two fucking Jews. The woman already looking like a mother-in-law and the man like an associate professor who would never get tenure.

"We're here, that should tell you something," Minnie said.

"Y'all late." Scratched himself lower, the crotch of his blue jeans beneath an oversized belt-buckle and boots polished to a high shine. Minnie had an expression like she wanted to spit and Earl hadn't changed from a sleepy kind of indifference. Like he was deliberative and slow and generally not in a hurry. Gestured into the room with the hand holding the suitcase and Artie thought must have been a heavy case to handle one-handed. "Y'all come on inside."

They passed him and the room looked like a modest motel room. Reasonably clean and the bedside table was scuffed and water stained. Smelled like old cigarettes and a thick carpet that absorbed odors from transient guests and their pets. The bed wasn't slept in, and room didn't give the sense of having been inhabited overnight.

Earl shut the door and latched it, and they had their back to him while he did. Room was chill like the air conditioner had time to work. There was no phone by the bed, only a lamp that wasn't turned on with a drab yellow shade. Earl took a seat and sat with his legs spread wide. Had his suitcase by his boots. Artie sat with his legs crossed and wished he had found a better place for the gun.

"Y'all ain't my usual clientele," Earl said.

"We're revolutionaries," Minnie said, "not some drug dealers looking for a pistol to keep with them while they sell dope."

"Well, suppose I've heard of more Jews in that line of work than I have of Jews dealing drugs."

"Why do you think we're Jews?" Minnie asked. Artie thought she sounded like a caricature on an anti-Semitic radio show Father Coughlin and Henry Ford might've co-sponsored.

"I suspect you're playacting at revolution like Angela Davis," Earl said.

"Dr. Davis is a genuine revolutionist," Minnie said, "and we'd be proud to do half of what she's done for the Cause." Artie noticed that Minnie had this way of using political slogans like they were proper nouns, like she capitalized them when she repeated them. Hadn't picked up on that, until she was talking politics to somebody who wasn't part of their crowd. Came off as faintly ridiculous.

"I think that would amount to only getting your boyfriend killed," Earl said, "and maybe a vacation in the Caribbean afterwards. Boy, you ought to be careful before your woman lights your ass up."

There had been a stretch when their reading group didn't seem to do anything except discuss the ongoing saga of Angela Davis. Cops had shot her boyfriend and her boyfriend had shot a judge and Davis had bought the shotgun for her boyfriend and fled to Havana, and Artie suspected it had been this that gave Minnie the idea to buy guns in the first place.

"I don't think that's how she meant it to happen," Artie said. "At least, I hope it wasn't."

"After the Revolution, we'll be building statues of Dr. Davis, how the Soviets have," Minnie said, ignoring him.

"Suppose I'll be one of the souls building them," Earl said. "Be sure to get the afro right, Negro's whole appeal is sounding overeducated with a head of natural hair and only half that's something can show up on a statue."

"You're fixated on Negroes having to look like Negroes," Minnie said. "That's the whole of the Negro Question, it's all about them not looking the same as you."

"Naw, if Miss Davis looked like me, she'd be a proud member of the Ku Klux Klan and talking about how many niggers got to be killed to set the world right instead of white judges."

Earl was cool saying that.

"You're saying that Angela Davis would kill Negroes if she was white?" Artie asked.

"Hell no, because she ain't got the courage of her convictions now to do more than buy the guns somebody else uses to kill the poor bastard. And that's with the whole system behind her to keep her out of jail. Bitch was white, she'd talk all day and be afraid to do the least little thing untoward because she ain't spending hard time in jail for killing no nigger any more than she's spending hard time for killing a white man."

"And if you looked like Dr. Davis?" Minnie said.

"They'd have had to shoot me like Fred Hampton and I'd have used my dying breath to tell the Panther next to me that I shot fucking first and none of this innocent man jive bullshit."

"You're a man of principle," Minnie said. Artie thought that, despite meaning it sarcastically, she might not be wrong.

"I'm a man a couple years ahead of his time."

"You're a reactionary," Minnie was raising her voice.

"And y'all are old hat but just don't know it yet." Earl sounded as cool as he had at the start of the conversation. "But, figure y'all ain't here for no educating, so let's get down to nut-cutting time. Y'all brought the money, or is there something else in that briefcase the Jew-boy's holding onto like it's his momma's titty?"

"It's just the money," Artie said.

"Do you have our machine guns?" Minnie asked.

"Machine guns?"

"I said on the phone that we wanted machine guns."

Earl scratched his chin and his nails were clean and his short beard was neat.

"I figured you meant machine pistols," Earl's tone warmed. "Course, strange to want machine pistols instead of something heavy like an assault rifle. An AK'd even be Commie, suit what I expect by y'all's complexion and conversation and general demeanor of your politics. Now, an AK ain't accurate for shit but it looks mean and you can't abuse it so bad it won't fire."

"I meant machine guns," Minnie said.

"Couldn't do nothing with machine guns, even if I got you some surplus M60s. Would need a team of you to manage the bastard, feeding the belt and hauling ammo and setting the whole thing up. Why, if you was trying to rob you a bank or some other similar way of drawing attention to yourselves you couldn't move around with a machine gun unless you got some real brawny types you chose not to bring with you today. Because this one here," and he gestured to Artie, "ain't got it in him to handle one. And that ain't even considering the problem with how much ammunition you'd burn. No ma'am, machine guns don't make no sense at all."

"That seems reasonable," Artie said. Felt like he ought to listen to an expert.

"We want something that can kill pigs," Minnie said, "and machine guns kill pigs."

Earl shook his head and his shoulders were set still and his eyes didn't blink so the effect was owlish. "I'm happy to facilitate y'all pulling the trigger on some policemen," he stressed each syllable of that last word, "and machine pistols will do you fine. Not as fine as some assault rifles, but then I'd need to meet you again and someplace else because those mothers don't travel in a suitcase."

"Are you trying to fuck with us?" Minnie said, and Artie thought she was trying to sound like a Panther. Only Jewish and shrill instead of Negro and intimidating. Minnie was operating under a racial handicap even if she was never going to acknowledge it. Though it couldn't be entirely racial, Artie thought as the Israeli girls he had met when he was playing kibbutznik for a summer before graduate school hadn't suffered from this shortcoming, and he'd been fucking afraid of them even as he'd been trying to hump them.

"Minnie," he said.

"No ma'am," Earl said. "Nice thing about working with white folks is that we don't rip off our customers."

"Would throw us all into gas chambers how the Germans did," Minnie said, turning the subject to the Shoah.

"White folks don't kill our customers, neither. Least not unless they really goddamned deserve it." Earl was smiling now and had straight even teeth and Artie thought that wasn't quite so right. Didn't have a smile like a hillbilly.

"I didn't come here to be threatened," Minnie said and neglected to include Artie.

"We didn't come here to be threatened," Artie said. "Not as though we are, of course."

"I ain't threatening nobody. I'm telling you that I, as a white man, am generally opposed to killing my customers."

"Because you wouldn't make any money off of them. That's all a fascist like you would care about."

Artie did think that this one might actually be a fascist. Not in the sense that the president of J.P. Morgan was a fascist, or the men who built the bombs to drop on Hanoi were fascists, but in the sense of being frank about being a fascist.

"Well, would think some Jews would understand about wanting to make money. Y'all came here to make some dough, and I'm a Southern boy and came North to seek my fortune there."

"It's going West to seek your fortune," Artie said, his teaching assistant instinct kicking in.

"Ain't Dixie, so it's all the fucking same to me."

Minnie was gripping her purse with her pistol in it.

"We want to see what you did bring us," she said.

"Happy to oblige, so long as I see the money."

Artie could not get the gun out of the briefcase without the fascist noticing. He would have to just hand him the briefcase, and Earl would find the pistol as he examined the wads of bills. Was a stupid goddamned place to keep his pistol, and Minnie had told him at least four times to put it there.

"Guns first, then the money," Minnie said anyway.

Earl stood up and stretched. Had more than a hundred pounds on Artie whose summer on the kibbutz hadn't put muscle on him. He flashed a genuine smile that was whiter and straighter than it should have been.

"Suppose I ought to've expected being Jewed on this one," he said.

Took the suitcase in one hand and put it on the bed and heard the slats creak. Had a four-digit combination lock set to 1-7-7-6 and undid the latches. Opened the suitcase and he brought the machine pistols.

"Got you MAC-10's. They're illegal as black-tar heroin and don't shoot worth a damn, but they look badass and are reasonably portable. I'm suspecting that's enough to suit your purposes."

Artie thought they did have respectability to them.

"Are they loaded?" Minnie said.

"Sister, do they look like they got a clip in them?"

Minnie turned on a dime and was trying to be smooth about it.

"Then when do we get the ammunition?"

"Soon as you fucking pay me."

"You have it on you?"

Earl eyed her and took his time. "It ain't in this room. Ain't so far away would need to make another trip."

Minnie nodded and was looking at Earl like he ought to know his place. Artie thought she'd never much cared for the proles. The Negroes were pitiable but white trash was boorish and didn't have the excuse of being Negro. Artie didn't much care for them either, but at least he appreciated that he was supposed to and recognized the personal failing.

"Artie, give the man his money," she said.

Artie handed Earl the briefcase with the money and decided the pistol would have to be an inadvertent gift made out of social embarrassment like putting too much change in the tip jar.

"I'm going to use the powder room," Minnie said. "We've got a long drive and I'm not stopping on the way back with guns in the car."

"Minnie, are you sure?" Artie asked.

Minnie ignored him and took her purse to the bathroom and shut the door. Earl watched as she went in.

Earl opened the case and the pistol was in the tear-away liner like a smuggler and Artie had felt clever about that. Earl missed the gun and checked the bills. Saw was all the right denomination and could see the satisfied math in his head. Walked over to Artie, didn't lower his voice.

"You fucking that one or did I guess wrong saying she'd kill you when she killed her boyfriend?"

Artie swiveled back to look at the door like it might swing open and then back to Earl. The motion didn't take any time at all. "Why do you ask?"

"You present like two people used to fucking each other."

"We're married."

Earl looked puzzled like he was trying to solve a small but bothersome problem with the way of the world.

"I didn't think y'all were the marrying sort. Too old-fashioned and something ordinary folks get up to."

"We, well," Artie wanted to say they had a relationship where they were free to sleep with other people and really it was Minnie who was free to sleep with other people, but instead, Artie decided to retreat into theory to get away from that reality. "By liberating love and labor, we can create a self-regulating worker's society." Artie didn't believe that recycled Reichian psychoanalysis, but he was still fluent in it. "Before the abolition of marriage has become universal, there are pragmatic social and legal advantages to outwardly observing the retrograde forms of sexual regulation."

"So what you're saying you might be Communists but you still Jews got to please your parents and it helps with your taxes."

Artie hated this man, because that was the plain language of it.

"You don't got any better-looking bitches?" Earl said.

Artie didn't have anything he could say to that.

"I suppose pussy's the same. But, still, got to deal with all the rest of it. At least, I'd bet you got to deal with all the rest of it."

Sounded like he didn't have to deal with women. And Artie assumed he didn't. He decided, knowing that Minnie was about to come out, to speak his mind even if that still came out limp and nebbish.

"You aren't a very kind man."

"I ain't, but then neither are you."

"I try."

"You're sheepish around people you'd like to kill. That ain't kindness, it's just weakness calling itself kindness to live with itself."

Artie wondered, genuinely, if that was true and realized it sounded like Nietzsche. About right, a genuine fascist echoing Nietzsche and his teeth weren't right and he might have actually read him. Artie had heard the books read better in the original German.

Minnie opened the bathroom door then, holding her pistol, and Artie was looking at Earl who had a knowing expression on his face like he wasn't surprised.

"That's a fucking lady's pistol," Earl said.

Then Earl slammed Artie like a defensive lineman hitting a blocking bag and Minnie pulled the trigger and nothing happened. Earl took the pause to cross the distance between them. Shoved Artie, who hit Minnie hard and the gun was on the ground and so was Minnie, and Artie was on top of her, and Earl was on top of them both. Artie was out of the pile after taking a hard elbow to the face and added a dent in his nose to the cracks in his ribs.

Minnie looked worse for wear very quick into the confrontation. Would've screamed if Earl didn't have a knee on her throat.

Artie had adrenaline and the blood was pumping out of his nose. Was out of the pile and there was a pistol on the floor but it was on the wrong side. Other side of Earl couldn't get to it in time. But Artie remembered the pistol in the briefcase. Scrambled, had the briefcase open and money in those neat stacks from the bank on the floor as he was ripping away the liner getting the gun, and Earl was turning toward him with his weight still on Minnie.

Artie wasn't faster than Earl but he had the head start and had his gun on Earl and the bullet would cross the space between them faster than Earl could even if he did move too fast for a man his size. Would be like shooting a tiger before it could pounce.

Earl didn't look too worried and Artie's adrenaline receded and he didn't pull the trigger. He wondered if the safety was on. Wondered where the safety was. Wondered what a safety was.

"You want to bet your life that whatever nigger sold you that gun took better care of it than he did the one just jammed?"

Minnie spluttered and Earl pressed his knee into her neck.

"Lucky for you. That lazy nigger's the only thing kept this bitch from shooting you in the back."

Artie felt the blood on his upper lip and had phantom pain in his back along with the bad pain in his ribs. Earl kept talking and this time to Minnie.

"Bitch, I'm going to lift my knee and you make a sound louder than sucking wind I'll fucking smash your head in."

He stood to his full height and moved to Artie quick and proud, like he was loping and arrogant and Artie thought he should shoot him now point-blank and most likely the gun wouldn't jam and the big redneck who might've been playing a redneck would die with a slug in his stomach.

Artie also knew he couldn't, however much he needed to. He suddenly understood those Jews who had waited in nice orderly lines waiting their turn so the Germans could shoot them on the Eastern Front. They fell in nice orderly lines into the mass graves. Germans didn't even have to throw the bodies in, Jews were polite enough to fall right in themselves.

Earl took the gun out of Artie's hand.

"That's a good Jew-boy."

Artie felt like he was back on the kibbutz with the tanned hard IDF veterans telling him he was a soft American Jew in their Sabra English. They were right.

Minnie turned on her side and was retching and Earl moved with the same arrogance and took the lady's pistol which hadn't settled the matter between them how Minnie and Artie had expected. Earl gestured with the lady's pistol to Artie.

"Now, why don't you sit on that bed and why don't this bitch sit with you. Y'all can comfort each other."

Artie didn't get off his knees until he was on the bed and Minnie kept broken eyes on Earl while she crawled to the foot of the bed. Her face didn't look like it had at the start and Artie thought she would need another nose job to adjust the one which had been her sixteenth-birthday present.

Artie helped her up and wondered if they'd get a divorce if they lived through this. What would they tell the judge? That she was willing to shoot him? He wasn't willing to shoot the man had beaten her half to death? Probably should amount to cruelty either way. Or they could move to California how they'd been talking about doing, live in the better weather and get one there, call it no-fault.

Could imagine a brighter future even if he was probably about to end up with a bullet.

"Y'all don't got any more guns on you?" Earl asked and was like a shooting-the-shit question. Artie shook his head.

Earl said that was real good and put the two guns in the chair and then took the case with the unloaded machine pistols and put the guns in with them. Checked the safeties and then closed and locked the case.

"Think y'all will understand that the sale's off. I'll be keeping the money and the guns you brought for having bruised my knuckles." Earl walked around so he faced both of them. Looked them over and looked pleased with himself. "I really ought to kill the shit out of both y'all."

"You kill us," Minnie said through broken teeth with a wheezy sound like her lungs were popped, "then law enforcement—"

"Bitch, if you ain't picked up on this yet, we're operating well outside the law here. Wouldn't count on those police you trying to kill to get you your revenge."

Minnie spat blood and it dribbled down her chin with the rest of the blood on her face.

"You really ought to get yourself a better attitude," Earl said. "Me and your significant other was having a nice conversation before you chose to try to come out shooting with a poorly maintained firearm. And like I told y'all, being a white man, I only kill my customers if I absolutely got to."

Minnie wiped the bloody saliva with the back of her hand and smeared across the bottom of her face.

"Keep looking me that way," Earl said, "and I might have to reconsider my decision to restrain myself."

"Don't," Artie said. "She doesn't mean anything. She's just upset. She won't do it again."

Earl took one hand and rubbed his elbow with it and the gesture looked like something a man might make riding a horse on a prairie that still had Indians raiding across it. Was a man who could kill them both and had reason to do it, and the gesture was his reconsidering whether restraint was the wise choice.

"Suspect it's more out of a lack of means than a lack of desire," Earl said.

Minnie couldn't crawl to Earl let alone fight him. Artie wanted to say something decisive like that. Something to communicate just how little he wanted to die and how it shouldn't be for his wife to decide.

"She hasn't got it in her to try again. And like you said, we're outside the law here. Nobody's bringing the pigs into this."

Earl finished rubbing his elbow and Artie knew he'd made a decision.

"Believe that's the truth."

Artie breathed as easy as his bruised ribs would let him.

"You ever wonder," Earl asked, "how it is that Israeli Jews are badass and their American cousins ain't worth a bucket of warm piss in a fight? Think it's being surrounded by pissed off A-rabs that does it, out in the desert where there ain't nothing forgiving, burning the softness out of everything?"

"I think you've said something racist, anti-Semitic, or misogynistic in every other sentence since we've met," Artie said.

"And I think you perk up when your bitch can't talk over you."

"That's probably true."

Earl laughed at that and Minnie didn't. Didn't matter much, kindling added to the brushfire sweeping through their marriage that morning.

"Suppose y'all weren't thinking, but it might've occurred to you that you'd be short ammunition had you managed to shoot me today."

Artie nodded and Minnie kept her broken stare at him.

"We might have used the money we saved to buy the ammunition separately," Artie said.

Earl looked at him like at least it was an honest answer, even if it was a fucking stupid one. "Y'all ain't well-suited to your line of work."

"No," Artie said, "we aren't. We can't all be suited to violence."

"Think that's what I'm well-suited for?" Earl asked and the question sounded like Artie was missing something.

"I'm not going to pretend I know what you're suited for, but we aren't suited to the same thing."

Earl whistled through his teeth, and his gray eyes had flash to them.

"Got me a Jew to admit he don't know what's going on. Ain't that something."

Artie realized Earl was having fun.

"Well, I'll tell you my understanding of myself," Earl said. "Now, my grandmother had a little Indian in her. Long time ago, she told me I was a coyote. You know what a coyote is to an Indian?"

Artie barely remembered his American folklore seminar and shook his head because he wasn't going to hazard an answer.

"Coyote was the god of chaos and knowledge," Earl said. "Knowledge like the Fruit of the Tree of Knowledge of Good and Evil, and he brought death and fire into the world. He's generally lazy and gluttonous, but when he got a wild hair about something he goes after it with a peculiar style and cleverness. He's what makes us know there's something to being alive and it's knowing that there's something to being alive that makes us appreciate that we are going to die."

Artie nodded his head because it sounded familiar, but Minnie was political science and didn't seem interested in anything except her own hate and ragged breathing.

"Now, took me some time to figure out what the fuck my grandma was talking about. But eventually figured out what she meant, and it ain't just that we all wild animals here, though that's a part of it. You understand what it means being a coyote?"

"Means you're smarter than you let on," Artie said.

"Jew-boy's catching on. You figure out the rest of what she meant, might even be glad you met me. Though I don't think your bitch's going to get that point herself."

Earl walked over and took the suitcase he'd brought with him in one hand and the briefcase they'd given him in the other.

"Now, I'm going to be leaving y'all. Would recommend you clean yourselves up some before hitting the road. Look bad enough you'd scare your own reflection, and room's paid up for the day under her name."

Earl walked past them. He unlatched the door and Artie knew he needed to ask a question before Earl left. He was damn certain he would never see Earl again but would spend quite some time thinking about him.

"Why are you letting us live, really?" he asked.

Earl raised the hand with the briefcase to his chin and scratched his beard.

"Because I sure am a coyote, and when it suits me in my coyote way, I like to practice what the hippies called consciousness raising, even if my methods ain't the ones they'd subscribed. Hell, my goals ain't the same either, seeing as peace and love can suck my ass." Earl opened the door to the world outside. "But hippies never did appreciate that there ain't no more than a cunt-hair between what'll learn a man something worth knowing and what will kill him stone dead."

Earl took the money and the guns and left.

Artie and Minnie sat on the bed. Minnie wiped her bloody hand on the comforter.

"Artie, go to the front desk and call the police," she said. "I don't have the voice for it."

Artie turned his head to her and the motion hurt his ribs. "We're not calling the police."

Minnie was looking at him dead and hateful. He thought, she might have tried to shoot him again if she still had a gun. Minnie would have written letters denouncing her own neighbors had her grandparents never left the shtetl. Hell, she'd have told the Germans there were Jews in the attic if she'd been blonde. She was a revolutionary because she liked telling other people what to do. She was with Artie because she liked telling him what to do. This time, however, Artie stayed put, and she didn't get up. They sat together bleeding onto the comforter.

# Bully Worship

Cole's childhood bully Bobby was paying his tab. "Can't tell y'all how happy I am to have gotten married," Bobby said to his friends as they walked out of the bar. He stayed behind to finish his last drink.

Bobby was wearing a wedding band and a class ring, expensive watch, khaki shorts, a red polo shirt, and loafers. Was beer gutted. Had always been fat, but he wasn't so fat as he used to be, and his skin had cleared up. Looked prosperous and suburban.

Cole, who was visiting his hometown from the city and having a meal on his own, had restrained himself until hearing about the marriage. Bobby sounded so goddamned happy.

"You remember me?" Cole asked when he got to him.

"Who the fuck are you?"

"Cole, from school."

Bobby looked him up and down and his eyes were bleary from the beer and seeing Cole didn't sharpen his focus.

"Sure," he said, "how you been, boy?"

"I've been doing good," Cole said. "But that isn't why I'm here."

"You ain't hitting on me, are you?" Bobby said. "Because I got to tell you, I ain't interested."

"You did like calling me a faggot."

"Ain't you one?" he said, and sounded like now he remembered who he was talking to.

"That doesn't goddamned matter. What matters is that you should fucking apologize to me."

"What for?" he asked.

"You once took my clothes away and led me around the locker room on a leash. Fucking took me into the bathroom and pissed on me."

Bobby finished his beer and shrugged.

"Good training for a frat."

"That's your excuse? You were fucking bullying a boy smaller than you and couldn't fight back, and that's what you've got to say?"

Bobby told the bartender to reopen his tab and ordered another one while Cole sputtered at him. Bartender asked if Bobby was being bothered, and Bobby said he appreciated how he took care of a regular, and that it was no trouble. Cole was repeating how he'd been defenseless and couldn't fight back, continuing on a similar theme.

"Could have bit my nuts off," Bobby said and started his next beer.

"What?" Cole asked, startled out of his stream of thought.

"When I had my pants down to piss on you, could have bit my nuts off."

"That was what I was supposed to do, fight you? Bite you in the manhood?"

"That was exactly what you were supposed to do," Bobby said and sounded like he was enjoying himself, "if you weren't such a little bitch-boy."

"I ought to hit you."

"You ought to," Bobby said, "not that you will."

Cole felt his hands hanging by his sides, heavy like weights he couldn't lift.

"You're still a goddamned bully."

"Sure fucking am," and checked the time on his expensive watch.

"I ought to tell your wife what you are."

"You think she doesn't know?" Bobby said. "Wouldn't be married to me if I wasn't."

"Can't stomach that you're fucking happily married on top of everything else."

"Came over to spoil my night, didn't you, boy?"

"No," Cole said. "Came over because when I heard you say that you were happy for getting married, I felt happy for you."

That caused Bobby to blink his bleary eyes.

"Hated you for feeling good for you," Cole continued. "Hate you for lots of reasons but one of them is for feeling good for you."

Bobby put his beer down and reached out and put his hand on Cole's shoulder.

"Well, that's mighty decent of you."

Silence. The world passed between them.

Cole started again.

"You're still a bully."

"I'm true to my nature." Bobby sounded knowing and drunk. "How you're still somebody's bitch-boy, ain't you?"

"I am."

Bobby started pressing down on Cole's shoulder. Rings dug into Cole's shoulder.

"Ought to thank me," Bobby said.

"For what?"

"For teaching you the truth early. Saving you getting above yourself."

Was like a harsher kind of meditation. Flagellation. Cole knew his arms were by his sides and accepted he wasn't going to lift them. World was still passing and supposed he had brought this all into motion and having bought the ticket was going to learn what was at the end of the ride.

"Thank you," Cole said.

"Ought to say sir, talking to me, boy," Bobby said.

"Thank you, sir," Cole said.

Bobby released the pressure and patted Cole's shoulder like he might a pet.

"That's real good, boy. Now," Bobby said like he was reaching the point of the exercise, "you still happy for me?"

"Goddammit, but I am still happy for you."

Cole had a funny expression on his face like realization.

"Why you think that is?" Bobby asked.

"Because we arose together, sir."

Bobby had a satisfied expression on his face that expanded to fill the empty world.

# WABI-SABI

Irma was chain-smoking her way through her two packs a day, and she kept the cigarette in her mouth while she rearranged the flowers in the vase.

The flowers were deep-red double-petaled peonies which Irma grew in her garden beside the pole beans. The peonies in the vase didn't match the peonies on the vase, but those were in a chinoiserie blue which didn't grow natively or anywhere at all. Those flowers were a color unique to mass-produced Chinaware.

The vase was blue-white China, and had a crack running down it from the lip to the base. The crack took a sure enough path to the bottom, for certain stretches slanting to the right and along certain others slanting to the left but always staying resolutely vertical. It was a thin crack at the top and widened toward the bottom.

The water Irma poured into the vase leaked out through the crack, and the drops of water would slide in ones and twos along the glazed exterior of the vase and across the

China-blue peonies. The drops would pool in the matching bowl which Irma set the vase in.

She settled the arrangement how she liked and couldn't have said why she liked the flowers in one way or the other except they were right in that moment. She thought was how the flowers ought to be and when the water got so it needed to be replaced, then the flowers would need to be some other way too because the world had changed around them, and their arrangement ought to reflect that change.

She stepped back and looked over her work and took a deep drag.

Irma's grown son Carl was sitting in a wicker chair and had watched her fool with the flowers and her cracked vase. Carl worked at the automobile plant a county over. Made good money, even if the folks who ran the place were Nips. He had talked about how he worked for white folks, but Irma knew that there were Japs at the head of everything at the plant because it was a Japanese automobile company. Irma's husband had died fighting the Japs during the war. Not the second husband, Carl's father, the one she had divorced, but the first one, the one Carl didn't know about, the one who had been very young and about to enlist in the Marines when he asked her to marry him. She had been very young then, too, and pretty enough, and he had gotten on one knee and it would've been impolite to refuse a boy who didn't know he was going to die on Okinawa. And now Carl was working at a Jap plant, and earning good money, and sending her some. She wasn't so proud as not to spend the money, but it wasn't right either.

"You going to wreck your health smoking that way," Carl said.

Irma thought he never did have something positive to say.

"Ain't worried over my health."

"Why not?"

"Smokers don't give a shit about their health," Irma said and took another drag before sitting down in the chair near her son. Exhaled the smoke in a long stream.

"That's a backward way of looking at things," Carl said and waved off the smoke. He had made a point of quitting when his daddy had died from cancer after spending a few years with a hacking cough. Carl hadn't taken the dying well.

"You talking like something that comes last comes first," he continued, "acting like you couldn't get to caring about your health. Like you is stuck how you is and couldn't get some other way even if you wanted to."

"That is exactly what I mean."

"Well, what about your flowers?" Carl asked like he might have found something his momma might care about enough to miss if she was dead.

"After I croak, the flowers'll go with me."

"Still talking like things all the way out at the end have got to happen."

"You saying I ain't going to die if I ain't going to smoke? You saying the cure for winding up dead is putting down my cigarettes?"

"No, momma, that ain't what I'm saying, only, don't have to hurry it up and smoking'll sure enough do that. And then those flowers ain't going to have nobody to water them."

"All I got's either going to go to pot before I do or get thrown out anyway after I wake up dead one morning."

Irma blew more smoke and watched the vase seep out its water into the bowl. Carl didn't have nothing to say to that because it was true and Irma wasn't a lady to try and bullshit about things working out better.

"Going to spend all your money," he said. "Ain't going to send you no more if all you do with that money is smoke."

"You make plenty money at the plant to spare some for me."

Irma had considered telling Carl why he shouldn't work at that plant. She'd decided after thinking over the subject through a couple of cartons that she wasn't going to explain after too many years.

She had been working in a munitions plant in California and her first husband had been of California, and after he died and the war ended she left the plant and got on a Greyhound bus and made her way back to the county of her birth and that was where she stayed.

Irma had started smoking during the war. Had steadied her nerves. Never lost the habit, or the nerves that needed steadying.

"I know I make enough to spare you some, but, well, can spend what I give you on things other than cigarettes. Like a new jug for your flowers that ain't practically broke in half."

"It ain't broke," Irma said.

"That's you being bullheaded. You just can't admit that you broke something and are being too stubborn to get another one that ain't broke."

"I weren't the one put the crack in it. Was that nigger maid you forced on me knocked it over. Even after I told you I could manage on my own without needing a nigger woman would wreck my house trying to clean it."

"You fire the poor woman?"

"I fired her black ass before my vase hit the floor. But, I suppose she did serve some purpose."

Irma started a new cigarette and stubbed out what was left of the old one before pocketing it. Was the sound of water filling the bowl.

"Cracked it," Irma said like she was thinking over something. "But didn't break it. Ain't broke."

"Could glue it back together, keep it from leaking," Carl said.

Carl had halfway hired the maid because he'd got to worrying he was going to walk in and find his momma two weeks dead when he visited her.

"No, I ain't going to do that. Would ruin it."

"It's ruined how it is," Carl said and sounding exasperated, "spills water."

"Bowl catches the water."

"Got to empty the bowl and refill the vase. All that's doing is adding work."

"Ain't such a hardship. And makes me take the time to appreciate what it is I got."

"You got a cracked jug." Carl seemed frustrated at her for keeping something broke and for firing the maid even though she probably needed the help and for plenty of years leading up to both those things.

"I have got a fine-looking vase."

"With a crack running through it."

"A fine-looking vase because it has got a crack through it. Why, ain't nobody else around here's got one of those. Makes it an original. A vase that has got some personality to it."

"Going to crack in two and spill water on your floor," Carl said. "Might be you'll slip on it."

"I'll clean up the spilled water. Done it plenty of times," Irma said.

"And the jug that's two parts instead of one?"

"When it breaks apart so the parts of it can't be put back together, I'll throw the parts away."

"That don't make no sense at all. You going to let it break in half so you have to throw it out even though I thought you liked having it."

"I sure do like having it. And when it's time for it to get gone, I'll sure hate losing it. But I'll have had it, and every time till then that I see it I get reminded I won't have it so long."

"Act like a goddamned Jap sometimes, momma," Carl said. "Harping all the time on how everything's goddamned going away."

"You ain't around enough to know what I'm thinking about all the time. And I ain't a goddamned Jap. I'm a woman from the middle of nowhere who's gotten goddamned old."

"Still talk in goddamn riddles like they do. Don't even got the excuse you don't speak goddamned English."

"Ain't said nothing that's a riddle. Been real straightforward this whole conversation."

Carl started like he was going to stand up from his chair and hurry out the room and slam the screen door behind him how he had plenty of times before. Stopped himself though and Irma kept blowing smoke and looking at her vase through the dissipating smoke. Vase held her attention better now than it had when it was whole.

"Ain't nothing I do's a mystery. Least not to myself," Irma said and was distant.

"What do you do with it during the night?" Carl asked.

"Let the bowl fill up."

"Don't it overflow?"

"Not no more. I've got so I got a feel for how much water I need to put in so the bowl don't fill up."

"Don't the jug or the vase or whatever you call it," Carl said, "don't it empty out at the same time the bowl fills up? Like it's more-less empty except maybe some water gets pushed from the bowl back through the bottom of the vase?"

"Vase does empty out. Ain't entirely dry but it ain't full of water when I get to filling it again the next morning."

"Can't be good for the flowers."

"They don't live long anyway even with water. Only taking a little time in bloom away from them." Irma's cigarette shook in her hand and was as much expression as she allowed herself. "And I stay up with it. Flowers don't go without for so long as all that."

"Could have the maid come to fill it. Save you needing to get up."

"No, she ain't going to do that. It's something for me."

"Could arrange the flowers for you, save you having to fool with them."

"What I'm doing takes feel, and a nigger maid knocks over a vase sure don't got that kind of feel."

"Did manage to break it somehow so that you like the vase more than when it weren't broke," Carl said. "Stands to reason, such reason as there is to any of this, that would take some kind of feel, might be as much a kind of feel as it takes to arrange flowers."

"There's a difference between arranging things so they look nice and knocking things over so that they accidentally get to looking better than they had."

"Think that's you trying to make something different, but you got me too damned confused to point out why."

"All I know is," Irma said, "she ain't coming back and she sure goddamned ain't touching my vase again, or my flowers neither."

Carl said sure momma and that he'd talk with the maid.

"You free to talk to her, but she ain't doing nothing with my vase."

"Yes, momma, I understand."

Irma and Carl sat and Carl had his head in his hands for a time while Irma continued doing what she did whether he was there or not.

"Ain't sure what I'm going to do with you, momma." Carl didn't take his head out of his hands.

"You'll put up with me until you put me in my grave."

Carl said he supposed that was true and sat back in his chair. He wasn't overjoyed and he wasn't as dispirited as he had seemed with his head in his hands. He told Irma that he'd keep sending her some money and Irma nodded and said he ought to stop complaining about how she lived what life was left to her.

"Yes, momma, I'll be sure to do that. Ain't going to be bothering you no more about the smoking or your vase."

They sat together with the water drops going down the vase and the bowl filling with water and the smoke claiming its part of the air in the room. Carl left after a time and said he would be seeing her soon, and Irma told him she'd better get the next wire same time she always did.

"I'll be sure to, momma, and I'm hoping I'll see you soon."

"Suppose the Nips ought to give you a day off sometime," she said. "Least they got to give you Sundays, because this is America and that matters something here even if it don't mean nothing to them."

Carl said that sure was true and that he wondered if the Japanese gave themselves Sundays off in Japan. "Seems like they might not know what to do with themselves, not having something to do that day a week."

"Folks manage, best they can," Irma said before realizing she'd come near to saying something kind about the Japanese and adding, "even the Nips."

Carl left after promising to wire the money next payday and visit, even if there weren't a date attached to the visit. Shut the screen door carefully behind him before walking out onto Irma's porch, getting in his Jap car, and driving back to the next county over where he had settled near the plant.

Irma sat in her chair and chain-smoked and looked at her vase. She counted time in the water drops down the side of her vase and the cigarettes burnt to their ends. She didn't get out of her chair until it was time to replace the water again, and she rearranged the peonies until they were how she liked them.

Her joints were bothering her and she was moving slower than she once had. She took her deep drag admiring what she had done, and she sat again with her cigarettes and her vase that would continue its cycle. She remembered California, and her first husband getting down on one knee, and that moment in time.

The smoke from her cigarettes dissipated in the room. The sound of the tender stream from the bottom of the vase filling the bowl with water. The drops of water along the glaze in their ones and twos. The deep-red double-petaled peonies against the blue-white China peonies, and all things arranged how they ought to be in their passing moment.

# Foreign Legion

Andrew Gilchrist finished the novel. It was a serialized thing by an author claiming a French name. It had first run in a men's magazine, which Andrew bought from the newsstand when he had enough to spare. For lack of funds, he had missed the beginning of the novel, and parts of the middle at irregular intervals during the original run. The novel was about the Foreign Legion fighting a sheik in the Sahara, and there was an Arabian princess who fell in love with the commanding officer, and she looked very much like the high school girl who worked the soda counter nearest the plant where he worked but dressed more revealingly.

Andrew placed the book on the shelf next to a line of books with similar titles and settings. Some were set in the South Pacific and some were in the antebellum South, and many were set in the War Between the States, but they all came out similar to the others. He took a backpack containing such clothes as he would need and some toiletries and none of his personal effects which he wouldn't be able to take with him all the way, and he put it over his shoulder and walked to the bus stop and waited in the heat of an East Texas summer. He stood in the direct sunlight rather than going under the awning of the bus stop because he was practicing.

Had his passport in his pocket next to his wallet. Passport had come in the mail earlier that week.

The bus went to a depot, where Andrew transferred to a long-distance bus, and he rode all the way to Houston sitting straight as a board because that was practice as well. The doctor's office where he was headed was a little general practitioner that Andrew had pulled out of a phone book and took a time to find.

When he arrived, the doctor was a short man with slicked back hair and a stethoscope and saw Andrew at the time of the appointment. Andrew handed him the paperwork that had been given him by the lady in front. Doctor read through the forms and asked what brought him there.

"I've got a place to be and I got to get shots before I get there."

Doctor asked where he was going, and Andrew said overseas.

"You running away from home?" doctor asked.

Andrew said he was eighteen and so it wasn't really running away from home.

"Just moving away."

"You trying to enlist?" doctor asked.

"Why you think that?"

Doctor shrugged and the stethoscope moved up and down as he did.

"I gave physicals during the war," he said. "Draftees and enlisted men. You remind me of the boys trying to enlist and lying about their age."

"You think I'm enlisting or that I'm lying about my age?"

Doctor said he thought Andrew was doing both and that he ought to strip so they could get the examination done.

"I don't need a physical. Need to get my shots."

"You need both if you're enlisting. Need a clean bill of health and between hookworm and hunger, boys like you ain't as healthy as Hollywood thinks you are."

Andrew took his clothes off because it wasn't wise to argue. Doctor wasn't entirely wrong, even if he didn't have a way of knowing that Andrew was doing something more than enlisting in the regular Army or even the Marines.

Doctor looked him over and not so long into the physical said there was something.

"You know you got flat feet?"

"Sure I do. Always had them."

"Didn't doubt that you'd always had them. Suppose I ought to have said, you know you can't go into the military with flat feet?"

Andrew said that wasn't going to be a problem and his voice was louder than he meant it to be.

"I ain't going into the military," he said, and doctor looked at him like he was lying, and he added, "I'm going into the French Foreign Legion."

"Don't know that outfit particularly," doctor said like was a novel variation on a common theme, "but unless they will take a boy who is an American 4-F, you ain't getting in."

Andrew said that their standards were harsher than the Marines and he was quoting the book he had finished that morning and doctor said that meant he wasn't getting in.

"You can't lie for me?" Andrew asked, like that was something he could request.

"Can't hide flat feet," doctor said like it wasn't such a strange thing to ask.

Andrew got his shots anyway. Was behind on them. Doctor charged him for the exam.

"You sorry for what you have done to me?" Andrew asked.

"I ain't sorry and I ain't not sorry. All I'm doing is telling you the situation as it is."

Andrew paid with what he had saved, and for it, wouldn't have enough money for his magazine. Then he got on the bus back to Houston. Didn't sit so straight on the way back. Unpacked his bag and put what he had taken back where it belonged, and was as though he had never gone but for what he had learned and the money he was out.

Andrew started crying and kept crying for a time, until he cried himself out. Got the book off his shelf that he had put there that morning and started back from the beginning. Read deep into the night until he fell asleep and dreamed of the high school girl who worked at the soda shop near the plant, dressed like she was an Arabian princess.

# MEDEA GOTHIC

She could tell Hyatt wanted a way out and the children were slowing them down. Kept slicking back his hair with his hands and looking across the hotel room with the single shaft of sunlight cutting through the gap in the soiled curtains to see himself in the bathroom mirror like he was trying to look good for the mug shot. Had all the money they'd gotten out of her brother in the trunk sitting out in the room like bad vibrations. Was one of those old-fashioned steamer trunks and had bad-taste gold tracery stamped on the fabric, white cotton bolls on imperial yellow stalks climbing along the sides of it against orange fabric that had become dull with time.

The money looked small in the trunk because Moira's brother hadn't raised all he might have. When she had put her clothes in she had imagined all the money they were going to have filling it up until it overflowed. She was also being practical, as she and Hyatt were leaving and she needed a place to put her clothes after all. Even though this whole adventure was real romantic, she had a common-sensibleness about her.

Had her husband's gun in the trunk as well, on top of the loose cash.

Hyatt was a salesman based in the city and selling in the rural counties around the city. Had started out selling encyclopedias and after he got tired of those he remained in the book trade for a time selling Bibles, New King James with illustrations that looked like watercolors you'd find in a hotel, and finally he started selling insurance. Had a new route for insurance which took him through Moira's diner regularly enough that they started to recognize each other.

Moira liked that he was a man with an interesting profession. Before she had got married she'd wanted to be a secretary because that had seemed romantic, working in an office for a big man in one of those high-rises pictured in the magazines. Had put that aside when she got married and only later after she'd started earning a little in tips she had stowed enough away for the correspondence course for shorthand and typing advertisements in those same magazines. But even after completing the correspondence course Moira couldn't write using those squiggly shorthand characters any faster than she could write using regular letters. And the family's old typewriter had been around since before the Second World War and wasn't real suitable for learning to type on.

She'd told Hyatt of her professional struggles when she was letting him buy her milkshakes all those times after her shift ended at the diner. She had started back to work there when the family was real hard up. He'd been so nice he'd buy her boy and girl ice cream or a slice of pie when they were hanging around. Got so he'd give them a ride home in his new red Ford T-Bird. Then he and Moira could drive off somewhere else if her husband weren't around, and most nights he wasn't. Hadn't been for the children getting born Moira might've been able to follow her older brother into the city when he went to college on scholarship instead of staying where she was and getting married to her husband, and they'd all have saved plenty of trouble.

First time she let Hyatt buy her a milkshake he had asked about her wedding band and she had told him the truth.

"My husband came back from Korea not entirely right," she said, "and with a medal didn't get him any money more than a niggardly disability pay he spends on beer. Got me pregnant when I was thirteen and the other before I was fifteen. Means I feel all wore out and I am not twenty yet."

Hyatt had told her she sure didn't look wore out and she liked him saying that and meaning it too. Had a sip of the milkshake when it was served by one of the waitresses who gave her a look like she ought to be careful with herself.

"Now, I never much liked my husband," Moira said and raised her hand like she was swearing to it. "My daddy liked him because he had a little money in his pocket and steady enough work. Trained him as a mechanic in the Army and hadn't gotten caught up in Korea would have done nothing except being a mechanic. And after his time being a soldier he went back to being a mechanic and drinks like he's going to die and has no time for me."

Had another sip and leaned over the counter to reach the straw, made sure Hyatt could see the curve of her figure.

"Think my daddy liked how he had been in the war," she went on. "I never did see much to admire about it. If he hadn't of volunteered would've drafted him anyway, and went in thinking he was a mechanic and saw combat because they were getting chewed hard by the Red Chinese and they had to throw everybody in. I can't see rewarding a man for something he had no choice in doing. All that is doing is calling necessity virtuous, and there's a kind of lying about that."

Hyatt said sure enough like he wasn't paying attention to what Moira was saying. Hadn't been in either of the wars. Flat footed. Said that to her sheepishly, how he was about his service record or the lack of it, and she said that was good on him.

"You spent the war making money like smart folks," she said, "like a man on the make."

"I did well enough for myself," Hyatt said. "Always more a body could have done, but don't let it bother me none."

"Sure," Moira said, "can't let yourself be all resentful stuck in the past when you got a future ahead of you."

Now, in the hotel room, Baby Gus was acting like he was going to wet himself. Boy had always been high-strung like he was entitled to delicate nerves while she had to struggle and get aged and wore-out and lose her looks young from being poor. Was sitting on the bed and both his legs were shaking so hard, really did look like he was having to hold it in. Moira thought that was so funny she said it to Hyatt. He didn't laugh and so Moira said it again and Hyatt told her to shut up and he hadn't ever said that to her and then Baby Sister laughed. Baby Sister had been lying on the bed with that one little bit of sunlight going right through her belly. She had always been close to dumb how little she spoke. Even that first day had hardly been excited about driving to a new town and staying in a motel, which should have been something special what with their never having enough money to travel.

And now they were on the third day and her husband's money and his gun were in the steamer trunk.

What had happened to start was they had called her brother from a filling station pay phone near the county line.

Moira's brother was the only member of the family had any money. Gone to college on that scholarship and made something of himself and never let the rest of them forget he was the one was made of money. Had a wife who he thought was good looking even if it was obvious she dyed her hair, and a big house could have fit Moira's family without intruding on him. He had more of the stuff than he needed and he was real stingy with it when he weren't paying for the country club where he played golf with men had even more money than he did.

Wouldn't even send any money to his mother without her practically begging him for it. Only paid for her funeral after the family held out the prospect of her going into the potter's field, and he had hardly spoke to the rest of the family since momma had gone in the ground in the cheapest casket which the funeral home would sell them.

Moira had always been resentful of that stinginess, how she'd resented Baby Gus being high-strung. Was all the same kind of superior attitude, while she was losing her looks taking care of her children and the house and working at the diner and trying to better herself.

And now Baby Sister up-and-laughed after being so superior herself by being petulant and mopey and quiet. So Moira hit Baby Sister hard enough that Baby Sister didn't start laughing again and started crying instead.

"Why the fuck you do that?" Hyatt said and he hadn't cussed at Moira before. "All that does is get her balling her goddamned eyes out. Folks next room get to hear her through these walls ain't more than cardboard and wallpaper, and that bitch manager starts onto us and, goddamn, would be a short trip to the gas chamber what we done."

Baby Sister was still crying. Balling away like she didn't care about getting the authorities onto her momma. Hyatt told Moira she needed to shut that bitch up.

"Honey, I'm not sure what I ought to do," Moira said.

"You'd better shut that fucking bitch up because, goddammit, it's a straight trip to the gas chamber we get caught."

Moira had first suggested them robbing her brother's two-story home, when they were first making a plan. But Hyatt had explained that folks with money, lots more money than a person needed for himself especially if he was stingy, folks like that didn't keep it around their houses. She had said that maybe he'd raise the money if there was a real good reason, so Hyatt had suggested that they stage a kidnapping. She had told Hyatt while they were courting that her brother had a soft-heartedness for the babies in the family, and had expected Hyatt to remember her saying that when the time came. Wasn't as though her brother would say no even if he didn't care particularly for them.

Hadn't been anything getting the children to take a car ride. Had taken them plenty to that fly-specked grease-slick diner, and Hyatt had just kept on driving past the diner. Moira had started on how there was a surprise for them at the end of the drive and weren't it so pleasant being in such a nice car with the air-conditioning on.

Now, Hyatt said the goddamned unit in this room needed more kick to it. Even without letting the sun in the room was heating with the still dead air inside getting heavy like a blanket. He started going on how the trunk didn't have the kind of money in it could get them far enough away could outdistance the law, not with the kind of law they were going to get after them. Might even rule in the first degree. Didn't understand the law well enough to understand the difference except the first degree meant there was no point in rehearsing a speech for the parole board laying in your cot because they was going to kill you sooner than let you out of jail.

They had drove the kids to that filling station and stopped and that was the moment the plan was real and hard because prior to making that call at the filling station pay phone they could have driven back to the diner and said was all a practical joke and the children would be scratching their heads until they had a slice of pie in front of them and then they wouldn't care at all.

All the plan took to become the real thing was Hyatt, whose voice Moira's brother wouldn't recognize, calling on the phone saying he had the children and needed a hefty ransom to ensure their release. Moira had the phone number on a slip of paper and beside it some rough figuring she had done about how much money she thought he could raise.

Her brother asked why weren't they calling the children's father. Was perhaps in the nature of an ill omen but there's bound to be resistance at first. Man takes a shock hearing how he got to give over plenty of money to save his loved ones.

"We're rich," she told Hyatt after he hung up the phone. They had been listening at the receiver together. "Ain't that exciting? Buy ourselves all the things we ought to have."

"Sure thing, honey, sure thing," Hyatt said.

Because they had to give her brother time to raise the money they had told him to expect a call in the early morning on the Saturday that was two days after the call and would meet him for the exchange before noon. Moira had said they would spend some of their money on a fine-dining city dinner to celebrate their starting their new lives together. Also meant dragging out how long they would be stuck with children, carrying them like dead weight.

Baby Gus had always been the smarter child, might've helped he was older, but Moira knew Baby Sister didn't have much between her ears. Why she was still crying and Moira hit her harder this time and made a wet sound and the wet sounds Baby Sister had been making stopped.

Moira turned from looking at where Baby Sister was lying still and quiet and Hyatt was looking at her like he was in a different room or one separated by glass. Like things kept at a zoo in the reptile house, the snakes that have their little glass boxes and children could annoy them by hitting on the glass and the signs telling them not to do that and them taking no notice because no one liked snakes and was more fun for the children to bother them than to let them be.

And was no consequence for bothering a snake behind glass or danger in watching it. Wasn't something could bite you unless it got loose or you reached your hand into the glass box daring it to bite you.

Hyatt was being driven by necessity, thought Moira, and while all folks at all times are driven by necessity, most of the time most folks are not conscious of that.

Hyatt had known plenty of motels from his route, but they had decided was smarter to go somewhere he was unknown. Moira had also been concerned that her brother would be cheap and make some calls to the police and sheriff's departments all around hoping to save himself his money, and he would brag about all his connections, so Moira and Hyatt couldn't count on the police and sheriffs dragging their feet.

So, they were left here, this stuffy and airless room in a motel off a county road that was dying because the traffic had started taking the new highway and so in a sense it was a victim of progress. Had an old-fashioned wood porch went in front of the rooms continuous like a frieze, and marks and chips in the wood. Doors with their numbers that were dull green-rusted copper. Sign advertised cheap rates and air-conditioning, though that turned out to be more-less a lie.

Had a clerk who was young and resentful with pimples when they checked in, and Moira had told Hyatt walking out with their key how much handsomer he was than that boy who like as not would die a virgin. Hyatt shrugged. Had his pistol tucked in the rear of his pants and his shirt loose over it. Said might be so and Moira told him to stop being so distracted. They met the manager and Hyatt got the trunk through the door. She came asking if they needed anything and didn't say anything about helping manage the children who were standing on the porch looking foolish and refusing to come inside.

Manager had that way how aged and bitter spinsters can make a charitable offer into an imposition. Had heavy lines around her eyes and a sagging neck and Moira thought about the creams and exercises she would need to keep from getting so she looked like that. Woman stood there in their room just for the sake of spying and Moira was sure she gossiped about the customers even if it took making up stories to make innocent folks sound dirty and lecherous. Manager asked if there was something wrong with their children.

Baby Gus and Baby Sister had not said a word between them.

She and Hyatt were sitting in the car alone now, with the children back in the room, asleep. They were talking about the possibility of having to use the gun.

"I suppose, well, suppose we wouldn't have to have used it," Hyatt said, "even if that manager threatened to call the police on indecency."

"Sure we wouldn't," Moira said. "All would take was showing it to her. Most folks, they see a gun and imagine it might be about to be pointed at them, they clam up real fast and start doing what you want them to do."

"How do you know that?"

"Don't take being a analyst in New York with a rich lady on a couch to know that is how the typical woman would respond to having a gun pointed at her."

Moira had toyed with the idea of getting herself a psychoanalyst. All the women in the magazines had analysts, they called them analysts to show they were in the know.

Hyatt said he supposed that was true. Still had the trace of a worried expression on his face like the impression on the next page after you bear down too hard writing with a pen.

"I been thinking, about what we got ourselves doing," he said.

"There ain't no need for you to do that," Moira interrupted. "We got every little thing planned out and from here on's just doing like we have already decided on doing. Everything's like a line cook on the breakfast shift making eggs for the ten-thousandth time, something can do without thinking."

"Well, that may be, but you're talking about the gun. I ain't sure."

"Ain't sure about what? Show my brother that gun to make certain he acts right."

"But what if he don't act right?"

"Now, the typical man the same as the typical woman will act right when a gun is pointed in his face."

"Then I sure hope your brother is a typical man."

"I'm sure he is. I have known him all my life," Moira said, "and I know he is a college boy who ain't never been in a fight and the only things he's ever liked are making money and acting superior. Why, he will probably make even more money because he'll be driven to get back what he owed us and he'll end up with more than he started with."

Hyatt said supposed that was true and didn't sound as certain as he might have. Moira reached over between his legs to check he was still a man. This took some of the bad expression off his face. Hyatt got satisfied and that took some more of the bad expression off his face, and then they went back inside.

Hyatt went to clean himself in the bathroom and Moira watched the color TV with the children.

After a little while, Hyatt came out in a towel and clean-shaved with his old-fashioned straight razor. Told Moira all of a sudden he couldn't stand to smell the children, said they must be going around in the same clothes for a week. Moira said he was wrong and didn't mention that she hadn't had them bathe the night before and had let them wear the same clothes going on two or three days in a row. Hyatt said even having them wash the clothes would still be soiled.

"God knows they been going around in the same socks and underwear like they're in the Army, out on patrols away from civilization."

"I ain't bathing them again," she said. "Then you're washing their clothes."

And so while Hyatt made sure the children didn't drown in the bathtub, Moira washed their dirty clothes in the sink with bar soap. Water refused to heat to anything better than tepid.

That night, she hardly slept thinking how even for the money she had coming to her, was still a goddamned nursemaid. Had the pistol under Hyatt's pillow, and the linens weren't clean and the pillowcase had splotches on it, but the pistol was oiled and polished and loaded. Before they'd turned off the light, she had told Hyatt he would need to bring the pistol loaded to the meet-up. Hyatt said that if he wasn't going to use it there was no point in loading it. She just explained he needed it to be loaded because if he knew it was loaded, he would act like it was loaded. Had to be convincing.

The next morning Moira was in a mood. What sleep she'd had was filled with dreams she would have to tell her analyst when she got one. Had been at crossroads and burying something at the crossroads, and had been flying through the air, and had been burying the old steamer trunk at the crossroads and had been flying out of the steamer trunk and had been buried deep underground in the trunk.

She told Hyatt all that at breakfast at a little diner nearby like the one she'd used to work at. Soon would be paying for all their meals at nice places and fine hotels and after they got settled someplace, would have a cook do the cooking for them. That was the future owed to her.

Their waitress was a brunette aged maybe sixteen, and Moira watched Hyatt look her up and down while she was talking. Would have talked about the money but they had the children. Hyatt kept eating his plain toast, taking little bites and sipping from skim milk and Moira asked if he wanted coffee and he said he didn't.

"Burns my stomach," he said.

"I've served you coffee plenty of times and never had no complaints."

"Why you needling me Moira, know full well this ain't like those other times."

"I ain't needling you. Only asking a question."

"You sure are needling me." He finished the milk and toast and didn't ask for more.

Children hardly ate either though Moira told them they ought to eat up.

"Y'all are growing and got to eat." Moira felt plastic saying that. Children ignored her how they always did.

She ate plenty and said that she wasn't going to let them spoil her appetite. Hyatt paid their bill and left a tip on the table and Moira was the last to leave and took the tip with her.

Was a pay phone outside the diner and Baby Gus was pulling on Hyatt who was already out the door before Moira caught up with them.

"I need to call daddy," said Baby Gus. "If he don't feed my fish, the fish is going to die." Baby Gus had a pet fish, which he won playing marbles at the fair. It came with the bowl and didn't do nothing but swim around but he was proud of it because he had won it.

"Might be your daddy ain't home now," Hyatt said.

"I can call the shop. It's Friday and that means he is working at the shop."

Moira said her son was being rude.

"You ought to say sir when you're talking to Mr. Hyatt,'" Moira said.

"But, momma, my fish is going to die."

"The fish ain't important."

Hyatt said he didn't have any change anyway.

"I gave the waitress all the quarters I got," he said.

"But momma took the money off of the table. She has enough I can make a call."

Hyatt stood like Moira had shaken him. He was staring at Moira like she was a picture had fallen out of a book, and the picture didn't make sense for the book. Like two objects were discontinuous and irreconcilable to one another. Like she wasn't a nice girl.

"He's lying," Moira said. "Goddamn little brat is lying."

"Give the boy a quarter, Moira."

Moira would not do that. "The fish ain't important," she repeated. "A fish doesn't have a life to begin with. A fish don't dream. All a fish does is swim in circles."

"Fish needs food," Hyatt said.

Baby Gus said that sure was true. "Sir," he added. Boy was clever.

"Moira, give the boy one of my quarters, and he will make his call."

The pay phone was wide and narrow like a picture at the movie theater. Her whole vision had concentrated that way and intensified.

"You don't want us to do what we going to have to do, do you Hyatt?"

"Suppose I don't. I think it's something strange you have talked yourself into, believing because it suits you."

"It might be strange and it might suit me, but it is also the truth. If my husband finds out where we are, he is going to kill us," Moira said. There would be no turning away, she thought. "God knows he has told me he was going kill me before."

"What're you saying?"

"I am saying," Moira said, breathed deep like she needed the air in her bellows, "that he has told me he was going to kill me and would say that after he was done knocking me around."

"He did that?"

"He sure did, threatened me plenty when he was on one of his drunks."

"Daddy never said nothing like that to you," Baby Gus said. "He never beat on her."

Baby Sister nodded her head.

Moira knew that the boy hadn't given a damn about the fish. Was planning on telling his daddy exactly where he was the whole time, just to deny her the money she had coming to her.

"He kept it from the children," she pleaded. "He likes them more than me. Loves them how he don't love me. Loves them how nobody loves me except you."

Hyatt hesitated and Moira saw everything hanging on him, and the whole world and all the time leading up to now, depended upon what he did next.

"Hyatt," she said, "if he finds out we gone off together, he will kill us both stone sober and will kill you first so he can make me watch, and I don't care about my dying but I can't watch you die."

Hyatt held her to him then, and the world was going to continue how it had, and the children were standing together on the edge of the curb.

"I ought to have protected you," Hyatt said. "Why didn't you tell me nothing before?" His voice was breaking.

Moira kept her tone sorrowful and confessional when she was so goddamned happy she could cry. "Never wanted you to worry about me."

"You never going to have to worry. You got me to protect you, swear I'll protect you."

Moira lowered her hands down Hyatt's back until the bottoms of them rested on the butt of the gun tucked into his pants.

"I know you will, knew you would when I met you. Knew what kind of a man you are."

There was no more discussion about the fish on the ride back to the motel. When they got in the door, Moira told the male clerk that she and her husband were going out for a little while and would leave the children in their room. Had her eyes on the phone by the clerk all the time she was talking and not only because one of the clerk's pimples was bleeding and unpleasant to look at.

"Just be sure the boy don't try to bum a phone call off you," she said. "He has got himself a bad habit of calling long-distance to a Yankee friend he met at camp, and if he gets through he won't get off that phone. Surely you don't want to have to put up with listening to all that and that manager-woman wouldn't be happy when she sees the bill."

Clerk said he'd be sure to keep the boy away. Moira patted him on the hand and said he was sure a nice boy and gave him a smile.

She and Hyatt drove into the little town nearest and started buying things.

Moira bought herself new shoes that had an impractical heel but looked real sexy and pearl earrings that she wore out of the department store. Had a new wristwatch and a purse on her arm, a heavy necklace that was thin oversized gold disks strung together, and a bracelet made out of one piece of metal that was beaten into a silver arc and a design like vines beaten into it.

Hyatt bought himself an oversized gator-skin wallet and Moira told him he ought to buy a new suit and tie and new shoes couldn't walk in comfortably how fine they were. Hyatt said would do that but that right now Moira was wearing most of the cash he had on him when they had left the motel and he couldn't afford all that just yet.

Ate dinner and Moira didn't take the tip, and then a double-feature drive-in and they couldn't have said a word about the second picture which started after sundown. Moira broke her new heel trying to get in the back seat and laughed when Hyatt threw it out the window and the other one too saying he would buy her a new pair and they startled a carhop who checked in on them. Hyatt bought a tub of popcorn and two Coca-Colas.

The second picture ended and they were satisfied and had managed to finish their sodas and hadn't touched the popcorn.

Drove back to the motel with the windows down and the night air and the motion of the automobile felt like freedom which is a soul becoming what it must be and has always been striving toward, and Hyatt walked in their room carrying the cold popcorn for the children as a treat and Moira said she would make sure they wouldn't be disturbed the next morning.

She walked into the office adjusting her dress so that it exposed more of her bosom and she looked up at the clerk like she hadn't been thinking of him before she walked in. Was the same boy with the bleeding pimples and he was leering and Moira thought, now, here was the kind of boy a girl can make use of.

"I just wanted to see if there were any messages for us," Moira said.

"No ma'am, there sure aren't," the clerk said. "That boy of yours tried to make a call like you said he would. Told him that guests weren't allowed to make calls."

He looked proud of himself, and mean. Sort of boy never had power over nobody and was a good thing he didn't.

Back in the room, Hyatt asked if she had made sure they wouldn't be disturbed the next morning. It took her a second to remember what she had said. He said they had forgotten to get a real dinner for the children. He would run and get them hamburgers and Moira said that was sure kind of him.

"I think I'll take a bath while you're out," she said.

After he left, she shut and locked the door and, ignoring the children who sat watching TV, went to the bathroom to run the water. Sat on the rim of the tub and undressed and put what Hyatt had bought her on the tile floor.

Baby Gus was too much of a sissy to accuse her of anything or say a word to Hyatt now that he'd been bested. Water was warm on her skin, and the water and the thought of the money put her in a fine state of mind.

"Boy surrendered," she said to herself, "all he got left is pity for himself."

She submerged herself up to her neck and her hair was wet and would curl and she would have it done soon by an expensive hairdresser who would know what to do with her hair that became unfashionably curly when it was long.

"Just like his daddy, a soul without the capacity for action," she said and she submerged her head under the water and felt like being reborn in the water which was the world before God moved across it and that was how the world was born.

The next morning, Hyatt made the second call from the pay phone. Moira watched him from the same booth in the diner they had sat in the day before. Had the same waitress who likely enough spat in their food. Didn't much mind as she let Baby Gus and Baby Sister have it and contented herself with coffee poured from the communal pot.

Hyatt, meanwhile, was leaning hard into the phone call, wrestling with it. Moira thought that was good because he had finally committed himself. At the end, it looked like he was sweating and his face was flushed.

He shuffled back into the diner like his feet weren't fully leaving the ground. Sat with them and didn't say anything and Moira got frustrated. She demanded to know what happened.

"I don't know," said Hyatt.

"He answered the phone," she said. "I could tell that much."

"I said I don't know. I'm not sure he is going for it."

"What do you mean, he ain't going for it?"

"I mean, I don't think he is going to get us the money."

"Why do you think that?"

"Because," Hyatt said, staring at his hands, "he told me he wasn't giving us any money."

"What do you mean, he told you that? Even for them?" She waved at the children and wasn't keeping her voice down either. "That bastard isn't giving us what we're owed?"

"Moira, he said he ain't going to."

Moira was out of the booth and out of the diner and at the pay phone and used the change she had taken out of the tip the day before to make the call. He picked up on the second ring.

"I don't know what you think you are doing," Moira said, "but I am dead serious that you ain't never seeing those children again you don't give us our money."

"Our money?" her brother said. He had a pip-squeak voice. How he had made something of himself with a voice like that was beyond her. "It's my goddamn money and they are your goddamned children. Moira, I don't know what goddamned stupid thing you're trying to pull by ransoming your own children, but nothing good is going to come from this and you aren't getting a penny from me either."

Whole world runs on necessity, Moira thought. Was no such thing as an unintended act because from the right perspective, which was God's perspective, all things had their perfect order and all things had to realize their own innate necessity within that vast order.

Her brother was still on the line. Moira said some more and kept on talking and her brother stopped acting superior. After some more talking, she told him that if he didn't want to deliver himself, then he ought to send her husband. He agreed to everything after that, said he would raise the money and send it with him. Hung up and had her hair long and curly from the bath and her bracelet with its silver-engraved vines knocking against the phone. She stood in the morning sun and her brother hadn't wrecked her. Hyatt hadn't wrecked her. Nothing was going to wreck her because she had her plan and the world had its plan and they were in alignment.

Walked back into the diner at her own pace and felt Hyatt and the children watching her like she was foreign.

“We’re having that meeting,” she said, and that was all she was going to say.

“Baby, why did you call him? Now he’s got to know it’s us doing this.”

“He already knew,” Moira said. “Besides, had to put some pressure on him, and I was the only person could do it.”

“But—”

“Ain’t no but about it. And he agreed he is going to get us our money.”

“Well,” Hyatt said and was looking at the children, Baby Gus confused and like he wanted to say something but knew better and Baby Sister confused and dumb. “Suppose at least we can get the children to him and take our money and be free of all this.”

Moira shook her head and the waitress came by. She ordered another full breakfast.

“We ain’t bringing the children with us,” Moira said. “All would do is hand them over and then all the law in the world could show right up and arrest us and we’d be put away right with nothing to bargain with. No, children going to be someplace else and he will only know where after we have left with our money.”

“But Moira, that ain’t the plan.”

“It is the plan, because it is the only plan that is sensible.”

“Where we going to put the children?”

“They can stay at the motel. Give the clerk money for a third day and we drive on, call from a pay phone near the state line and my brother goes and picks them up.”

“Leaving them alone,” Hyatt said.

“What we did most of yesterday and you didn’t have no complaint.”

Hyatt said he supposed that was true.

"We are going to eat and then we are going to go," she said, "and we have plenty time to drive to where we got to go, and the children'll go where they supposed to go. All of us end up where we ought to be."

Baby Gus said he wanted to know where they were going and what she was talking about.

"Momma's always been crazy," Baby Gus said to Hyatt. "Daddy tells us we ought to let him know when she acts strange."

Moira wanted to call him a bastard. She had been married when she conceived him but she had not meant the words when she had said them and the words didn't mean nothing if they weren't meant, because the words were directed to God and God knew when she was lying and that she had a good reason, and He would absolve her of the lie and of her marriage and of everything that came from it.

"Boy," Moira said, "you are going to get with your daddy real soon. That is where me and Hyatt are going to get you, and all it takes is you being patient and not complaining like you deserve something more."

Baby Gus ate just a little of his breakfast and Baby Sister did too, and Moira ate everything, and all Hyatt had was his coffee and when the children got up Baby Gus's legs were shaking like he was going bowlegged. He held Baby Sister's hand as they walked to Hyatt's car.

Hyatt drove them back to the motel and Moira paid for another day. Had the same clerk manning the office.

Moira told the clerk they would be gone for a little and back again, "But if you don't mind, my husband likes our privacy and so he would rather not have any maid come by. We promise we ain't making a mess of anything."

Hyatt was sitting on the bed with the children when Moira came in and she told him he ought to keep the door locked.

"God knows that manager," and Moira added, "We ought to make sure the children don't do nothing while we're gone."

Hyatt asked what she meant, and Baby Gus was shaking in that high-strung way of his.

"Please, Mr. Hyatt, momma's crazy," he said. "Me and Baby Sister'll be good. There ain't no need, least not Baby Sister because she's dumb anyway."

Hyatt looked at the boy and then at Moira and was dull in his eyes. The trunk was looking dull too in the room with the curtains drawn so only a little light came through.

"Hyatt, you got to tie Baby Gus's hands back. Boy'll run if you don't. And Baby Sister too. And if you don't put a gag in their mouths, they liable to start screaming and then where will we be? That manager'll find them and whole thing'll be ruined."

"Moira," Hyatt said, "I ain't doing that. They got nowhere to go and even if the manager does find them, won't matter none because we will already have our money."

"Then least got to put him and Baby Sister in the bathroom and get a chair so that it stops the door. Least that-a-way they won't be tempted and won't make a mess of themselves neither."

So Hyatt led Baby Gus and Baby Sister into the bathroom and neither of them complained. Baby Gus was smart enough to know he was getting off lighter than he ought to, and Baby Sister never complained. Put a chair under the door and Moira said through the door that they oughtn't blow out a lung screaming because their daddy would be by to get them soon enough.

"You attract the wrong kind of attention, you get actually kidnapped, and Lord only knows where you would end up if that happened."

"That ain't funny," Hyatt said.

"I don't mean it to be."

Moira had set the meeting at the old junior high where she had gone until her marriage, and which had closed after being ordered to integrate. She figured there was something poetical about having the meeting there.

They were there first how they planned and because the fence was busted, drove right onto the field and parked the car on the old fifty-yard line. Let the car idle and they sat with each other and Moira thought about the past and the future and she wasn't sure what Hyatt was thinking. Little while later, a truck drove past, then doubled back and turned onto the field. Was her husband's truck. Cherry red and vain. Didn't have the money for a new one, but he was a good mechanic and took care of it.

Hyatt said, "What's your husband doing here?"

Moira said, "It's all going how it ought to."

She told Hyatt they had better get out of the car. Day was approaching noon and the field was unmaintained and the scoreboard was rotted and the bleachers had rust in them. She told Hyatt to pull out the gun.

Her husband parked the truck at approximately the forty. He killed the engine and got out and by his step had been drinking. Moira had gotten expert at reading her husband and gauging how far gone he was. Was still recovering from the night before, approaching sobriety but not quite there yet.

Hyatt was pointing the gun now as her husband approached.

"I know you got a gun," Moira called out to him. "I know you got that sidearm on you which you took home from the service."

Her husband went down on one knee and whole body leaned forward and Moira wondered if he was going to try something fancy like pulling the gun from a holster on his ankle and firing in one smooth motion like a gangster or a detective might on the television.

But instead, he used his left hand to take the gun out of the back of his pants. Must've been something about men specifically, thinking that was the place to keep a gun when they didn't want folks noticing a holster.

"Step away from that gun now," Moira said. "You ain't got to stand near it like something might tempt you."

Husband stepped away down the field and Moira told Hyatt keep the pistol on her husband. She moved quick and took the gun off the overgrown green where he had been standing and aimed it at her husband while she backed toward Hyatt.

"Where's the money?" she asked.

"It's in the truck," he said and sounded like he had a hitch in his throat.

"My brother give you what he was supposed to?"

"Moira," her husband said, "he gave me what he could. I got what I could from your daddy and everything we had in the bank. It ain't so much, but it's got to be enough to get my children back."

"Going to give me every penny I got coming to me," Moira said.

"Your brother don't have the kind of money you always acted like he does," her husband said, "but we got something together, what we could for you."

Hyatt lowered his gun, but Moira didn't lower hers.

"Please, sir," her husband continued, addressing Hyatt, "don't care that you and Moira are running off but she's taking my children. She told her brother she would put them in a Mexican orphanage and I'd never see them again we didn't get all the money she asked for, and she asked for more than any of us had even all together."

"That isn't, we aren't going to do that," said Hyatt.

"Thought she had it in her," her husband said. "The goddamned bitch has evil in her."

Hyatt turned to Moira then, asked if they could talk, but Moira said this weren't the place. Hyatt kept on.

"Moira, what did you tell your brother? You tell him all that?"

"He's lying," Moira said.

"I ain't," her husband said.

"And my brother still would not give us our money," she said. "Would lie and say he ain't rich even though he has bragged about being rich."

"So we just going to take what is here and be on our way?" Hyatt asked.

"No, we got to keep a hold of the children. Otherwise we can't get the rest of our money. Why we couldn't bring them in the first place, because I knew my brother would screw us."

"I thought was because you were worried about the law?"

"Can do one thing for lots of reasons."

"And what do you intend on doing about him?"

That was when her husband started running toward them and had a knife in his hand. Moira knew the whole world was right.

Hyatt hit him in the chest with the pistol. Missed the first shot but the second hit. Inertia and desperate rage kept him going and Hyatt hit him twice more and he finally stopped. Leaked blood across the distance between the second and the last shot and made a puddle where he ended on the forty-five.

Moira walked past what had been her husband toward what had been her husband's truck, which was full of their money.

"Never meant to," Hyatt said, like he wasn't talking to nobody except maybe God. "I didn't even want the thing loaded."

Moira opened the front door and was a grocery bag in the passenger seat. Reached in to get it and stood on the running board with the bag on the driver's seat and what had been her husband's service weapon next to the bag.

"I didn't want to kill nobody," Hyatt said.

She started rifling through the loose bills and trying to count it only she kept losing her place. Had expected the money to come in neat stacks how it would if her brother had gotten it out of the bank.

"I never even wanted the goddamned thing loaded," he said.

Moira didn't look from the bag. "And it's a good thing it was, otherwise would be you bleeding and dead already and him starting in on me right about now."

Hyatt was sobbing. She was satisfied, money enough in the bag that it felt good to her. Considered it a good start and would get the rest from her brother in due time.

Took the gun and the bag and left the door open because would soil the interior and it is hard to hurt the dead but you can try. Was curious of something and walked over to the body. Man had pulled the knife from somewhere and looking saw the sheath for the knife looped around his ankle. He had been getting his knife when he had made that exaggerated motion putting down the gun. She was satisfied.

"Should have brought a second gun," she said to what was left of her husband, "but I know how attached you were to this pistol." Held it to him and considered firing into him for good measure, decided against because he was dead and she was practical and didn't want to waste the bullets.

Told Hyatt they had made enough noise and folks weren't close but ought to start driving.

"Where? Moira, we got a dead man and that ain't something we can run from."

"It sure is, and we are going to go to the motel and the children because we still need them, and in a couple days and a couple states we will make another call to my brother and he will know we are serious people."

Hyatt hadn't said much after that and had crying jags as they drove back to the motel.

"Hyatt, there ain't no reason to think you are going to be charged with anything," Moira said while she was driving because Hyatt couldn't manage it. "Why, you acted in self-defense."

"What kind of crazy are you, self-defense?"

"I'm not any kind of crazy and that is why I know you were justified. He was going to kill you and then me. Simple as that."

"And you had his gun, pointed at him, and didn't pull the trigger."

Back at the motel, she told him to wait a minute before letting the children out of the bathroom, and she put the money loose in the trunk because she imagined it would look so nice and full and put the gun she'd taken from her husband in as well. Children came back into the room and Hyatt wouldn't look at them as though he was trying not to think about them.

Instead, he was staring at her like she was a snake behind glass. With Baby Sister sullen and Baby Gus nervous and like he was going to piss himself.

"What are you doing back here?" Baby Gus asked. "Why ain't daddy here?"

"Boy," Moira said, "you had better keep goddamned quiet."

Baby Gus shut up and Hyatt started up.

"No point in lying," Hyatt said. "Remember you saying something about there not being no point in lying once it didn't serve no purpose."

"You saying that I have been lying?" said Moira.

Hyatt nodded. Was like he'd worked something out after he had finished sobbing in the car. "Think you planned all this, wanted your husband dead and wanted your brother's money."

"Daddy's dead?" Baby Gus said.

"I wanted you," Moira said to Hyatt.

Baby Gus had his head between his knees now, and Baby Sister was sniffling, confused. Whole goddamned motel room felt like a sweatbox and filled with crybabies couldn't appreciate how things had to be because the world wasn't cutting entirely their way.

"Sure you did, Moira, and I wanted you. But that ain't you denying the rest of it either."

Moira knew was going to have to tell the truth eventually because there was a dead husband lying on a football field at her old junior high, if he hadn't already been found and carted away. Like as not didn't have too much time before they had to start driving again. She'd have to tell the truth eventually.

"I am willing to accept people dying, if it means being with you and free."

"Free of what?" Hyatt said. "We were already free, could have left anyways, plenty of girls leave their husbands, could have acted like we was married and wouldn't, goddamn wouldn't have been exactly ethical but nothing nobody or God or Jesus would have trouble forgiving."

"That would have been lying, and I am an honest woman. Needed to be entirely free."

Was nothing now except the sound of Baby Gus crying and moaning. Baby Sister still sniffling and the hum of the over-strained and under-powered air conditioner. Moira knew she was having to communicate something that was central to why she had to get her husband on that dead football field before she left.

"Needed to be free of the dead hand of the past, Hyatt. Would have kept me here until the end of me."

Hyatt was a rambling man and she had liked that. He was a man selling until he had enough sold to be free of needing money and that was to Hyatt what her past was to Moira.

"Being free means your own soul being able to come out in the world as it really is," she said.

"Moira," he said, "you might be right. Might be the only way you were leaving and might be this is freedom." Moira hoped she had convinced him. Was showing him how the world was and that was preaching the truth.

Hyatt looked around the room like he had left the past behind and thinking of the future how Moira was, was searching for something and then went over to the trunk and opened it.

Was the first time he'd gone into the trunk and when Moira asked what he was doing he said they were going to need supplies for the road and needed money for that.

"You got plenty more money coming to you, least that is the plan."

"We have got plenty more coming our way," Moira said.

"Sure we do," Hyatt said, "that is surely true."

Hyatt said he'd take the car and drive down a ways. Needed food would travel well and a full tank of gas.

"I'll come with you," Moira said and was looking forward to getting out of the motel even if would have to drive back to get the children.

"No, you can't do that," Hyatt said and was firm. "These children left alone, they start shouting for that manager and that's it for us. You got to stay with them until I get back."

Moira bit her lip. Her children were slowing them both down.

Hyatt took loose bills from the trunk and stood up, looked like he was figuring something in his head and leaned down and took some more before he closed it. Moira thought must've been a generous amount and he was stuffing it in his pockets and his new wallet but then he did need to get everything to last them a while.

Hyatt walked past her to get to the door.

"Hyatt, I been thinking," she said. "Why don't we go to California?"

"California," Hyatt said.

"California's where folks who got a future go," she said. "There's all future there and nothing old, everybody's becoming somebody else over there like actors, how they can't here."

Hyatt said that was surely true. Moira leaned in to kiss him and he obliged. He had his hand over the pocket bulging with his wallet and opened the door, saying he would be seeing her. Moira closed the door behind him and heard the engine start and the car drive off.

Baby Gus was acting like was the end of the world, and Baby Sister was starting to get worked up again. Moira said they ought to be quiet and give their momma time to think.

Needed to figure, would have to make another call from somewhere on the way to California and would make the arrangements. Might be could have her brother wire them the money or, no, safer have him leave the money someplace like spies in the movies would, make him drive where she told him to go while they waited in a real nice hotel. Could have followed him to the city once and instead he was going to come to her now.

But would have the children with them. Would mean couldn't enjoy wherever they were staying no matter how much of their money they spent.

She stepped into the bathroom, realized couldn't even shut the door to the lavatory because Baby Gus might run off and start talking about his daddy being dead.

Saw Hyatt's straight razor on the shelf and was certain there was a reason why Hyatt shaved old-fashioned. Had put that razor at hand, and every tool had its purpose. Didn't need the children with them. Only needed her brother to believe the children were with them, a clean decision and inevitable.

"Kill your kin and only then will you find deliverance," she said and knew she had heard it from somewhere, maybe somewhere far to the east like Korea where her husband had won his medals and gotten so he would marry her, and so her marriage and her children from that marriage had come from the East and it was from the East they would return while she went to the West, and all part of the great necessity.

Stepped out onto the rotting porch after it was done, and was a bright day and the transition hurt her eyes. Only shading into the late afternoon and cloudless with a strong sun and all that had been happening would've thought more time must've passed because the world had changed.

Took her husband's gun with her. Put it in her purse along with the leftover money. Wanted to keep them out of the unclean room, and both had blood on them.

Money amounted to a few days of good living.

Walked to the office and was the manager behind the desk. Looked old and like the worst possible world, the kind of life Moira knew she wasn't going to be cursed with living.

She paid the manager for another day.

"You must be enjoying your time here," manager said to her, "keep adding days."

"I'm free," Moira said. "First time in my life I am free."

Manager acted like she hadn't heard her, might not have. "Well, your husband came by about half an hour ago and left a letter and asked me to mail it for him. Now, he didn't stamp it and it's a bit much to ask me to buy a stamp for him."

Letter was addressed to her father and she had a sour feeling as she stepped out the office. She ripped the top of the envelope open. Was a small piece of paper like notepaper left next to a phone to scribble messages. Was handwritten and it took her a moment to understand the cursive: *Moira. You have made a monster out of me. I might be going to die for what we have done but I'm not dying with you.*

The world and love had stripped her bare. Stripped away all that weighed on her and constrained her, and she couldn't be surprised by her fate.

She didn't walk back to the room. Turned instead and started walking down the surface road. She worked her thumb for any passing vehicle and weren't many on that stretch so took a while, but kept at it until she caught a semitruck. Man behind the wheel was about her husband's age and had a tattoo on his hand of a nude woman.

He told her he was headed two states away to the west.

Would go to California, thought Moira. That was where girls who were young and had their destiny in front of them went to become what they had to be even if they needed to dye their hair and change their names and noses. If she couldn't make it there she would make it to Mexico, but California was better. She got in the truck and shut the door.

Driver asked her what her name was. "Don't meet so many pretty girls and like the chance to get to know the ones I do."

She told him her name was, started to say Moira and caught herself and said Medea instead. Was a name she had read somewhere, a long time ago.

"Medea, ain't that a name," he said, "but sure is pretty."

He had the radio on and she told him he should turn it off. "I don't like listening to it, and I can keep you plenty entertained."

He said that sure sounded good to him and turned the radio off.

# FLOATING WORLD

Lieutenant Fant had been piss drunk and breaking orders on fraternization when he got pulled aside. He had meant to go from the sake bar to a brothel but was drunk enough to get talked by rapid broken English into attending a geisha house on the Gion. Had expected to be greeted by a bare-breasted Jap girl with her face painted white. Instead, a girl wearing a heavy red silk robe with blue trim shuffled him into a matted room with rice-paper walls and a three-part folding screen. Screen was taking up too much space in a corner, decorated with gold paper and a thrush on a bare branch painted across.

The screen caught the dim light from a paper lantern, and the rest of the room was in deep shadows. Woman had left and closed the sliding door. Lieutenant Fant tried standing and couldn't, and so adjusted himself. Couldn't sit how the Japanese did, forward on their legs. Wasn't shaped for it. Was the sound of bare feet on mats along the hall, and faint silhouettes moving across the rice paper, keeping time with the sound.

Woman in a kimono opened the sliding door. Brought a scent with her, perfume on a freshly washed and powdered body. Couldn't tell her face from the others, all the same to him and obscured in the dim light, but the scent was new and unique to her. Smelled like jasmine blossoms. Reminded him of Mississippi, and Ole Miss where he had matriculated before catching the end of the war.

Younger girl came in next, carrying a heavy teapot resting in a portable stove and balancing a black ceramic tea set.

"Tea," the woman said like it was all the English she knew.

"Sake," Lieutenant Fant said. Wanted to drink until he passed out, which couldn't be so far off.

"Tea," the woman repeated and sat in front of him in the Japanese style. The girl put her load between them. She bowed toward Lieutenant Fant and maintained the pose as she closed the sliding door.

The iron stove and ceramic teapot sat like void space between the two, the light from the lantern suggesting them like the barely visible circumference of a new moon.

The woman started preparing the tea and Lieutenant Fant said he wanted to get fucked. She smiled and showed blackened teeth and he was horny enough it didn't dissuade him, but her continuing with the tea preparation implied he wasn't getting any. Scratched himself in frustration. Said again what he wanted and slurred the words so it wouldn't be clear even if she did speak English what he was asking for, and the woman began mixing a green powder in a ceramic bowl with an irregular lid. Used an instrument looked like a horsehair shaving brush. Sound of the brush in the bowl reminded him of his granddaddy applying shaving cream before using a strop razor.

Grandaddy always said that he had whooped a Rebel Yell as Pickett gave the order to charge, and that the last step he'd taken was the farthest the Confederacy ever reached.

Lieutenant Fant wondered if this woman's brother or husband or father had shouted banzai on one of the islands. Had carried their empire forward with their charge. Torn down by overwhelming firepower, same as grandaddy's brothers-in-arms.

Younger girl opened the sliding door again and had an instrument in her hand like a three-string banjo with an unusual head. Sat behind the woman preparing the tea so she was almost flush with the sliding door and started plucking the strings. Was the emptiest sound Lieutenant Fant had ever heard, like a battlefield enough days later all the wounded had died or been carted away. Had he possessed sobriety, would have fled the room, and kept fleeing until he found a brothel and passed out on top of something small-breasted and for sale.

Woman kept preparing the tea as the younger girl continued playing. Three strings in an empty sky, and Lieutenant Fant turned away as though he might find more space for himself, though lack of space was no longer the problem, but rather the terrible emptiness of limitless space.

Tried focusing on the screen that was the only bright light in the room.

The scene was different. Were women in heavy makeup and heavy robes and men in funny hats standing around a palace, and the palace was on fire and horsemen were shooting arrows into the bystanders fleeing in flat relief. Was like the end of a cloistered world, of aristocratic pretensions and stylish illusions dissolving in the harsh light of the flames inked across the gold paper.

Was like a stylized portrayal of Hiroshima, or the burning of Atlanta as done by a Japanese.

Turned to the Japanese women who were the survivors of the recent defeat and he was the descendant of his grandaddy who had survived the earlier one.

"I got beat by the Yankees, too," Lieutenant Fant said.

"Tea," the woman said like she might have understood him and handed him the ceramic cup with a crack along its edge. Had water that was dark green in the light, and Lieutenant Fant drank it down and the taste was bitter and stronger than the sake, and the tea went down his gullet and the sides of his mouth, staining his shirt in the matted room at the center of a defeated world.

# MOTHER KALI

The carnival arrived on the outskirts of town with the sound of guitars. It was a little town and a traveling carnival, in a washed-out part of the Southland. The traveling carnival would cross the Southland on strumming guitars, and the little town stayed right where it was. The town didn't grow and only lost itself, its outer edges curling back as the tin-shacks emptied out for employment or vagrancy in the city and leaving it further reduced toward the center: a town-hall that was red-brick and overbuilt in its red-brick-and-copper, with the monuments to the War Between the States and both World Wars in front. The monuments had common last names engraved across their faces—the same families sending their sons to war every few generations, and the memorial to the Second World War had been newly laid.

Men who had little else to do sat and squatted on the courthouse steps and wiled away their time in gossip and chaw and chain-smoked cigarettes. There were guitars faint in the middle distance and their gossip changed from the foibles of the town's notables and Negroes who were respectively rich bastards and nigger bastards. Their conversation gained a rare expectant tone because the men with little to occupy their days knew the incoming carnival by its sound and though its schedule was irregular, it was always welcome.

"They got them the prettiest girls," one man started, and the subject was understood.

"Girls who will put a man in the doghouse," continued another who had been caught in a compromising position the last time the carnival had come through.

"Girls who will ruin a man and imperil his immortal soul," a third said, and didn't sound as though he had such fear of ruination or damnation as would prevent him from acting on impulse.

"Wonder if she'll remember me," a fourth said, and more men than would admit the fact to their wives wondered the same.

The carnival set itself out quickly. The tents and stands and stages went up, and with them their associated signs announcing various diversions and excitements and vices. Trapeze and circus acts and some rides for the children, and, more excitingly for their parents, the exotica. The adults-only freak show. The educational stalls which sold dirty books described as manuals for sexual health. And most importantly, and memorably, the girls.

Sheriff Burnham knew he ought to have run the carnival out before they had even put their trailers in park. The operation was more fluid and precise in deploying itself than an amphibious assault, because here there was the profit motive racing against the inevitable indecency charges if they didn't decamp ahead of law enforcement and warrants. Slowness of effort in the unfolding or the leaving and the whole enterprise would have been a waste of gasoline and human effort, exchanged for a few nights in a cell and perhaps an obscenity trial if the local district attorney was particularly aggressive.

Burnham had heard the sound of guitars, but he had been distracted from his professional obligations by fond and exciting memories. He had, in his youth and shortly prior to his enlistment, gotten thoroughly smashed on the shine, the carnival's high margin and high proof offering in a dry county. He had come to in a ditch with his shirt and wallet missing and a general feeling like he had been hit by a train. That his medical examination had found him free of VD had been a small miracle and left him reasonably certain that he had been robbed of his wallet before he had successfully traded away his virginity. It had been a rare night for a pastor's son and set the tone for later periods of wartime leave, during which he had always represented himself and his service well. Or, if not well, according to expectation.

Burnham had enlisted on his eighteenth birthday in the first full year of the war. He had been busted back to buck private once and ended his service battlefield commissioned to Captain Burnham. He had not ended his service a virgin. That condition had not survived long after enlistment, although it did manage to outlast basic training. He had returned home with his medals to a quick marriage to a pretty girl and election to his current office after the incumbent's still had caught fire. The controversy had made for a colorful campaign and temporarily enlivened the conversations on the courthouse steps, and after personally supervising the vote-counting with his service weapon on his hip, he had been reluctantly declared the winner.

Burnham had run on his record and the most recent conflict had left him with a patch over his left eye. He preferred the effect to a glass eye.

This was the carnival's first appearance under his tenure as sheriff. Game was that he was supposed to run the carnival out, which gave him a pretext to attend. As his boots were getting muddied from walking through the tracks stamped between stalls and tents, the first waves of guests having denuded the field which the carnival had occupied of its top layers of grass and soil, Burnham thought he must have been the sorriest goddamned son of a bitch in the world to have let this fucking degenerate show get itself established. Was an absolute dereliction of duty and if this town had any balls to it the voters would run him out of his job at the next election season. Not that they would.

Dressed in shirtsleeves and blue jeans without a visible marker of authority, he had been offered marijuana, pornography, a dice game, a stiff drink, and a woman, all by various agents trying to wave him into the appropriate tent or byway created by the labyrinthine arrangement of temporary structures. The woman had offered herself, barefoot in the mud, wearing a kind of long orange robe that was draped across her and wouldn't have been difficult to drop so her tits were showing. She'd called him sweetie, and, after his momma, who had died early, only women who charged by the hour ever called him that. Went strange with her heavy makeup and platinum hair. Burnham considered the temptation. If he weren't the type to be so tempted, he would have dressed official with a badge and gun.

Burnham had been the only son and only child of the town's late Baptist pastor. Having discovered one day that his son had scribbled drawings of Custer and Indian braves in the margins of the Sermon on the Mount, with Custer's blond coiffeur bloodied in crayon-red by a darkly penciled tomahawk, his father had accepted he was destined for a martial occupation and simply required that he attend weekly service until he had reached the age of enlistment. Now, the Battle Cross tattooed on his inner arm in blue ink was the residual of his faith and the memorial of his service. Believed in it more from the service—how a patriotic man might believe in the flag, and how a man in combat believed in the men beside him—than from the religion itself, though he possessed the language of his father's faith, as it had been incorporated into the rituals of the armed services.

The guitars were playing and there were various strands of them. They played against each other, modal and droning. There were ordinary guitars and steel guitars, but those weren't all and had become scarcer as the carnival had established itself. Had been replaced by foreign instruments. Guitars which had become long necked and thin bodied with a thick base and a bulbous head, played by intent men seated throughout the carnival grounds. Some were accompanied by hand drums, and a similar strange long-necked instrument, and others played unaccompanied. The performances lay on top of each other and put a man in a strange kind of a contemplative mood even if his heartbeat was being accelerated by what else was on offer.

Music was like a foreign religion intruding onto Southern custom, layering over it. The rest the carnival had on offer was aimed between a man's legs.

Burnham stopped in front of a stand crowded with townsfolk buying souvenirs. He picked a postcard off the rack. Was a coon card, illustrated with naked pickaninnies being eaten by alligators. One was up in a swampy kind of tree and the others were on the riverine shore and the gators were coming out of the green water, and the one in the tree was pointing down and laughing at the ones who were getting swallowed.

Burnham grinned and put the card back. Lady next to him whose Sunday dress was trailing in the mud was buying a complete set and the saleswoman was trying to sell her a second, because they made such a wonderful gift. She had a red dot on her forehead, and she was good at selling.

The next stand and sparsely attended was a book stall. Books all had covers like brown-paper bags and nothing on their spines. Burnham opened the nearest and it was a Tijuana bible, with the first page at random being a couple engaged in athletic and vigorous activity in three colors. The colors ran outside the lines and the lines weren't clean either, but he doubted that draftsmanship was highly prized or particularly important.

Down a ways and with the carrying sound of strange guitars and the chatter of the attendees, well-dressed gentry and shoddy white trash all spending their leisure time, was a raised platform like a small stage for a theater in the round. As Burnham approached, a man dressed in tails and a top hat climbed a portable stairway onto the stage. He was corked and shoe-polished like a cheap Al Jolson, and his face reflected the spotlight. The effect exaggerated the area around his lips, leaving them white. He started a performance of "Swanee," mugging and crooning for the crowd around him.

Burnham felt he was watching a cabaret in Germany just after the war. He remembered a German girl looking hungry and with her ribs showing, singing American show tunes as she stripped naked. Sounded like she had learned them listening to records a long time ago. She sang a Negro spiritual and clearly didn't know it wasn't meant to be sung stark naked on a stage. Burnham remembered how his limited sexual excitement had waned entirely after that and been replaced by something foreign, something he didn't remember from his daddy's preaching. Some sense that there was a great spirit to things, but it did not fit neatly. Had an unsettling quality to it, like the spirit of the world was an alien thing. Girl had stopped singing then and gone off with a clean and well-paid officer, and Burnham lost that feeling and would never reflect on it. Wasn't the sort of thing he was given to reflecting on.

Beside the stage was a tattooed man like he was waiting his turn. He was shirtless and wearing tights like a wrestler in a fixed match, and was posing as though he was practicing his routine. Could have doubled as a strongman, and probably did, overdeveloped muscles inked with tattoos. Flames and crosses, nude women and naked cherubs, Oriental women with flowing robes and Chinese symbols. Had a small crowd watching him and ignoring the minstrel. Some of the crowd that Burnham recognized as veterans had self-pitying expressions. Put to shame those men who had prided themselves on the solitary anchors, nude women, and crosses that were the permanent mementos of heavy-drinking nights during their periods of enlistment. Dressed as Burnham was, his tattoo was visible to the world as well. Didn't have shame that it was the only one on him.

Past a magic act using Chinese rings and dirty playing cards with the novelty that the magician was Oriental, a man was standing in front of an oversize poster taking up all of the side of a tent. Man was a town notable looking like he'd just seen

God. Burnham's angle of approach was such that he couldn't see the poster until he was practically next to the man. The letters describing the act were large in blue-and-red:

KALI DARLING

PROVOCATIVE AND EXCITING EXOTIC DANCER

WONDER OF HINDUSTAN AND TIBET AND FAR CATHAY

The dancer pictured was clad in two tassels and a G-string, and but for the blue tint and trick photography that gave her too many arms, would've been real terrific looking. Burnham found himself getting excited looking at her and had to adjust himself.

"Could give a man impure thoughts, and strange ones at that," Burnham said out loud.

"Think that is the intent," said the man beside him.

Burnham nodded to the man and whistled to the dancer on the poster. Even the smell of the place was overripe and humid, sweat and cigarettes and too many people getting excited.

The Chinese magician showed a young boy his card, the Queen of Hearts with bare breasts, and Burnham knew he ought to start arresting folks. He'd remembered that deck of cards from the last time this carnival had come through, that detail had preceded his taking a drink of something sharp like battery acid and survived the later alcoholic blackout. He thought it was a fond memory. Even still, was a law and he was nominally sworn to uphold it.

So Burnham walked over and told the musician that if he didn't put the deck away, he'd be forced to ship his ass back to China.

"Where the hell's the bastard runs this place?" Burnham added. "Need someone to pack this whole show up."

The Chinese looked at him blank and alien, though Burnham knew for a goddamned fact this boy spoke English better than he did. He then spoke in a high-pitched stream of gibberish. Started pointing at the poster and interjecting the occasional word of English. Burnham caught the words *see* and *dance*, as though they would meaningfully assist in rendering the rest intelligible.

"You got anybody here will admit to speaking English?" Burnham asked.

"Barker," the magician said, pointing past the tent, and far away was a man on a smaller stage, gesturing and looking like he was having an animated conversation with himself. Burnham couldn't hear a word over the minstrelsy songs and the guitars which were putting him in a strange mood, like the world might get swallowed up in their overlapping droning grooves.

Told the magician that he ought to learn goddamned English, and the Chinese played it straight, like he couldn't understand a word. Burnham respected that he didn't break character. Conveyed that respect by calling him a goddamned degenerate chink and told the boy had been watching the whole interaction that he ought to go find his momma before walking in the direction of the barker. Burnham's boots needed a high polish from walking through the mud.

The barker was shouting over the strange foreign guitars, had a trio consisting of both kinds and drums at the base. He was stationed near one of the entrances and was telling them that Kali Darling's show was tonight and to buy tickets.

"Y'all ain't going to want to miss the wonder of the Orient. Trained in the art of love in a monastery in Shangri-La. Fled the Red Chinese and found sanctuary in the harem of an Indian Raj. She has toured the capitals of Europe and the homes and bedrooms of the crowned heads of that continent. She has come to this country to spread her gospel in this New World she has yet to conquer. The loveliest, most dangerous woman in the world. The one and only Kali Darling."

Told them the price of tickets and added, "Adults only, you understand."

Burnham thought the woman must've had quite a career decline to end up where she was. A genuine slump. Worse trajectory than an actress has been declared box office poison and forced into summer stock theater.

Burnham stood at the base of the platform and called up to the barker to come over here. Raised his voice to be heard over the noise.

"And who might you be," the barker said like he was trying to work the crowd. Ones who knew Burnham inched away like they were afraid they might get hauled in themselves.

"The law," Burnham said, and barker's expression changed.

Barker announced his brief departure and give one final reminder to buy tickets before he scrambled down the steps.

Barker had a worn expression to him, and a stained collar and tie. Looked morose and fatalistic, like something he knew was coming but couldn't avoid. Like a train and he was tied to the tracks, or a bill collector who had his address.

"You the sheriff here?" he asked.

"I am."

"Suppose you want something?" he asked.

"I suppose," Burnham started without great enthusiasm, "it is my civic duty and obligation to run you out of town."

"Expect me to pack this up myself?"

"Don't care if you do it yourself or you get help, but this operation's got to clear out."

"Isn't up to me what we do." Barker reeked of high proof.

"Don't think you're understanding me. Y'all got to clear out or I'm obligated to start making arrests. Ain't out of personal desire so much as the gross indecency y'all got on display requires me to do it."

"They won't listen to me." Barker's general aloofness made him difficult to get a handle on. "The lady runs this show, and all I do is bring in the marks."

"What lady?"

"The lady," and the barker pointed to the poster. "Kali Darling. This here's her show. You want us to leave, got to talk with her."

"How about arresting you personally?"

"Wouldn't much matter, except to me. She'd keep this place going."

Burnham's eye kept flicking to the poster without meaning to.

"Suppose I could shut this place down by posting some signs saying closed by the county and putting you in jail to make a point. Would save me having to have another conversation."

"Look here," barker said, "could shut this place down and we'd head on to the next place and in a little while we'd be back here again because she'd say we are coming back here. Could throw me in a cell and might be doing me a favor because you'd get me away from her."

Burnham studied the poster. Lady had assets, even if she chose to portray herself in a strange color and arrangement.

"Ain't sure you'd want to get away from that," Burnham said.

"Getting away might kill me or it might save me, I sure don't know which because it is sure hard to tell with her."

Burnham looked back at the barker and the man had an earnest expression to him. Like he was too burnt out and worn through to have guile on the topic of that woman on the poster.

"Bitch sure has done a number on you, ain't she?"

Barker nodded and added, "She sure has."

Burnham had pity on the man. Might as well have a bit between his teeth and a bridle.

"Suppose I ought to talk with her."

"Think you should," barker said, "and would probably enjoy meeting a man like you."

"She would?" Burnham asked.

"Likes them big and a little beat up."

Burnham had never been slim and had gone slightly to fat now that he wasn't aiming to be a PT stud. Given he was taller than most, and with the patch over his eye, cultivated a particular impression that suited his personality and his occupation. That it sounded like it suited the woman on the poster wasn't an intention, but he'd done well with women since he'd started on them and it wasn't unsatisfying to hear.

"She ain't planning on sticking around long," the barker added. "She knows the game, just maybe plays a little different than you do. She got to dance once before she leaves. I think she likes dancing. Suits her vanity and her purpose."

"Might be I have to disappoint her," Burnham said.

"Might be," barker said.

Told Burnham where he could find her and Burnham told him he ought not to keep selling tickets for a show wasn't happening.

"Ain't never sold tickets for a show I knew weren't going to happen," the barker said.

Burnham made his way toward the trailers on the outskirts of the impromptu grounds, headed for the one the barker told him was Kali Darling's personal trailer.

Beside the trailer were a group of barefooted women wearing foreign robes, and he assumed they were whores like the others in that getup. The trailers were aged and rusting, and the weathered look of them reminded Burnham of a graveyard full of worn headstones. Aside from the poster taped to the door, Kali Darling's trailer was the same as the rest. Considered whether he ought to knock down the door to demonstrate seriousness or only knock. Decided ought to start reasonably friendly and progress from there. Called for her to open up.

Woman who opened the door was the finest bitch he'd ever seen and wasn't blue either. Wasn't wearing much more than panties and pasties, plus the exotica headwear. Had an oval-shaped metallic clip in her hair that rested on her forehead and a blue vein running along one tit that disappeared at the pasty.

She was looking at him with deep brown eyes, set with long eyebrows that he could, if needed, convince himself were natural. Her expression was like she had been expecting him and he might have made better time.

"You're the law," she said. Had teeth that could draw blood and wore something that smelled like sex.

Burnham said he was. She stood aside and raised an arm like she was directing him in.

"Suppose we have things to discuss," she said.

"I suppose we do," Burnham said.

Passed by and brushed against her going in. Wasn't much space in the doorway and she didn't get out of the way.

Had posters of herself, advertisements for her appearances at clubs in San Francisco and New York, and a vanity with an oversized mirror framed in lights. Had perfumes and makeup across the vanity, and a bronze-colored idol of a man dancing in a flaming circle. Had another and larger idol by the shuttered window. The trailer smelled like perfume and sex, and jasmine. Idol by the window was of a hideous woman, blue as Kali Darling appeared on her posters. Bright-red tongue lolling. Had a heavy sword and a head grasped in her numerous arms.

"This county has finally found itself an attractive sheriff," she said, as though that was the main issue. Her accent was like the boarding school accent of a girl that had dropped out well before graduation. As though learned but imperfectly mastered.

Burnham was stuck on the larger and more disconcerting of the idols. There was a fresh garland around the idol's neck. Jasmine vines. Had unsettled him enough he hadn't taken control of the conversation and had let her start on what she wanted to talk over. Feeling her as he'd walked by had first distracted him, and now this less pleasant distraction had overcome him.

"Do you know who she is?" Kali asked.

"Think that was outside of my religious education. I'm a Baptist."

"No, you aren't," she said with certainty.

"Well, I was baptized and my daddy was a pastor. And identifying heathen idols weren't part of his Sunday sermons."

"I imagine it wasn't. That's my namesake. An Indian goddess they call Kali."

"Hope I ain't insulting you when I say you don't look like her."

"It's not insulting at all, even if it isn't entirely true," she said and told him to sit down.

He nodded and took a seat on the couch, and she sat on the chair at the vanity. She turned the chair so she was facing him with her legs crossed.

"How'd you know I was the law?"

"Even if you didn't look like a sheriff, it's the sort of thing I would know. The criminal element and its discontents are close to my heart."

"Think that's having it backwards," Burnham said. "Criminal elements are the discontents. The law ain't."

"It's a matter of perspective," she said and Burnham nodded because this wasn't the conversation he needed to be having. "Kali needs her criminals. In the old days in India, she was their goddess. They'd worship her by strangling their victims."

"She ain't much for respecting the law," Burnham said, "any more than y'all are."

"We take after each other," she said. "And I suppose you're here to tell me that we're obscene and unwelcome in your county."

"Suppose I am," Burnham said.

"Don't sound so enthusiastic about it."

"Suppose it'd be easier to be enthusiastic if you looked like her," Burnham said. "Though I doubt you'd be drawing a crowd on your looks if you did."

"If I wasn't attractive, it would be easy to kick me out personally, but you probably wouldn't need to," she said.

"Unless you were making your money as a freak show instead of a striptease. But, then, would still have to kick you out, because we can't be having those either."

"Being unattractive enough is its own kind of obscenity."

"I ain't going to entirely disagree with you. Either way, you do need to get gone."

"And if I stick around?"

"Then I got to throw you in jail."

She wore red nail polish. Didn't have a ring on her finger, not that it would have stood for much.

"You would have me cancel my act?"

Burnham's eye kept wandering to the posters and the idol and the sweet-smelling blossoms circling her neck and breasts.

"You ever consider putting more clothes on?" he asked like a rear-guard action of a beaten army.

She removed her hand and uncrossed her legs. Flashed a smile.

"I make my living taking them off."

"I'm sure you do," Burnham said.

She stood and didn't have much to take off. Kept the clip in her hair.

After, she was running her red nail along the tattooed skin on his arm and tracing the outline of the rifle cross. All he had on was his eye patch. Had even gotten his boots off, were too muddied for her couch.

"I am led too easily into temptation," he said.

"It's only temptation if it's a sin."

"It is."

"In the East, there's a way of thinking, that screwing can be a way of praying. Emptying your thoughts so you can know something you're otherwise too districted to appreciate."

"No good-looking woman ever cleared a man's head."

"There is an acknowledged risk of getting very lost in sex, and becoming ruined."

"Sin enough you get yourself saved or damned," Burnham said.

"They like to stress that you need the right mentality going into it."

"Course they do. Or else we'd be animals."

"Tantra's always been a kill-or-cure way of living."

"Sounds like gambling for your salvation."

"A returned sinner has a higher place in heaven than a natural saint," Kali said, "because he has had to wrestle with greater demons."

Saying that, she sounded like his daddy, rehearsing a sermon. He could imagine his daddy having recited that very line, although he weren't sure his daddy would've meant it.

"I ain't never gone in for all that."

"Your God has to have violence in him," she said.

"You should talk," Burnham gestured toward the lolling idol.

"She has violence in her. But, Sri Ramakrishna worshipped her as a caring mother."

"Who the hell is that?"

"A dead, crazy, and loving monk who taught that we were all one with God."

Burnham scratched his temple and wondered idly if his pretty wife would smell the woman on him. "You ain't even Oriental."

"I'm as Southern as Vivien Leigh."

Didn't have the strength in him to get up and didn't much want to yet.

"How'd you come into this operation?" he asked, knowing it was still a going concern and would be for however long she kept an interest in it.

"I heard the guitars and knew this was my place in the world. Waiting for me. I made the guitars into sitars and tamburas. Added the tabla drums, too."

Burnham figured those were the funny kinds of instruments and did what he did with all the words she was using which he hadn't heard before, which was to ignore them. "How'd the old management take to you?"

"You met the barker?"

"I did," Burnham said.

"They weren't prepared for me."

"I can sympathize with that position."

"They get plenty. Even after my cut."

"Suppose you ain't selling yourself cheap."

"I know what my body's worth."

"Suppose we have both made our living with our bodies," Burnham said.

"I was dancing when you were overseas."

"Might have been dancing when I lost my eye."

"You get anything for losing it?"

"A medal for gallantry and a Purple Heart."

"You sold yourself cheap."

"I can't say I disagree."

"Sex pays better than fighting," she said with professional pride. "Only ways a woman can outearn a man are dancing, acting, and prostitution."

"I thought I was smart enough after the service to swear off strippers."

She shifted her weight and patted him on the belly. Had gotten pussy-gutted since leaving the service. Swung her legs and put her feet on the trailer floor.

"Doubt I'm the first man to misjudge himself," he said, staring.

She shook her head and he wondered if he'd ever get the smell of her off of him. Whole trailer was thick with the smell, and the vines around the idol.

"I think that you're a woman likes making men her dogs."

"I surely am. Kali takes her due."

"She sure does."

"If you want to keep on giving, can find a place for you."

Burnham rubbed his good eye and smelled his sweat and hers.

"Telling me I ought to run off and join the carnival?"

She said that was something like it. "Only you aren't so innocent as that sounds," she added.

"I ain't."

She rested a hand under her chin like she was trying to describe something she already knew. "You would make a good strongman. You have the right build for it, and it isn't so difficult for a man like you to put on that kind of muscle. Only have to be sure of what you're aiming for."

"Even if you're willing to put me on payroll while I lift weights to make something grotesque out of myself, I'm not the kind of man can fit here."

"You're a man who has known violence. That makes you the kind of man who suits Kali's Carnival."

"That what you calling this now?" he asked.

"That I am, even if I haven't put it on the poster yet."

"Was a soldier. Ain't the same as being a mad dog or a thug."

She laughed and Burnham wondered what part of that was funny.

Burnham could see himself by one of those stands, wearing nothing more than Johnny Weissmuller in a soundstage water tank. Would be like he was inflated, posing like the tattooed man. Have a crowd looking at him and some of the men and boys wondering if they could look like that, given time and effort and Dynamic Tension. Have this trailer to live in, and a wife several counties away until she managed to serve the divorce papers. For cause. Would be straight abandonment.

He wondered if he'd be happy.

She ran her hand across his stomach and rested it on the Soldier's Cross tattooed on his arm. Bright-red nails against the blue ink of the rifle, same color as the idol's tongue. She smiled at him.

He had already come near to dying. She was teaching a religion of driving yourself near to death and perdition and finding something right before the end and walking away alive. How an idol looked like destruction by violence could from another way of looking at things be motherly love.

He had lost his eye coming near to dying, and he had been wrong. He had gotten more than a medal and a Purple Heart. He had learned something.

"I'm happy in my line of work and satisfied with my wife."

"Well," she said and reached between his legs, "I doubt this will be the only occasion when we see each other."

"Won't be able to miss you, those funny guitars carry so far the whole town knows you're coming."

"They announce that Kali Darling is coming."

She stood and let go of him. Started over to where she had dropped her panties and pasties, and stepped into the one and put on the others. Burnham kept flicking between her and the idol, seeing them reflected in the vanity mirror. Gave the impression he was looking at one person from more angles than was usual.

"Why'd you start calling yourself after that?" he asked, nodding toward the idol to emphasize his point. She looked from the idol to him like it was the most obvious thing in the world. Had those brown eyes. She got in his lap.

"Because this is the Age of Kali. The Age of Destruction, and the Age of the Mother, and I'm a sign of the times."

"You ain't so modern," he said. He was going to give into her.

"I'm as modern as the atomic bomb. Was reborn when Trinity detonated."

"Where the hell did you pick up this act?"

"Between the barker and the poster, you've heard my life's story," she said. Didn't have any guile in her brown eyes. Were dark and loving. "At least, for this go around."

Didn't make any goddamned sense. He believed her anyway.

Later, as the sun began to set, barker announced that men with tickets should make their way into the tent for Kali Darling's show.

"Remember," barker shouted over the crowd and guitars, "this show is strictly for men of legal age."

Burnham knew the idol would be there before he got inside the tent. Tent smelled like sweat and mud, and jasmine blossoms. The idol was dressed with flowering vines in the center of the stage. Kali was wearing lipstick that matched her nails and the idol's tongue, saturated like Technicolor blood. Looked into the crowd and then down to him in the front row. Brown eyes rested on him, and she smiled. Sword slashing the air and the head held high, skin so deep blue that it was black, sucking all the light from the world, nothing of color except her red lips and lolling tongue. Was like watching an aerial bombing. Army films of a city full of Germans or Japanese catching fire. Like footage from Los Alamos. The explosion bubbles before turning into a mushroom cloud.

# ZHUANGZI BOXING

Spencer once dreamed he was a boxer. His body was trained and cut, in shorts and gloves. Perspiration slicked his skin under the ringside spotlights. The fight of his life. Simultaneously he was arguing with his manager. His manager had fixed the match without informing him, and Spencer had fought like it wasn't fixed. The argument and the fight going on at the same time.

His opponent was hazy and undefined, blurred by the lights and the internal logic of the dream. A fighter that was raised arms and legs dancing like Muhammad Ali. Spencer entered the ring.

Spencer threw a quick jab and a punishing hook. They fought and the rounds passed and the two were evenly matched. Spencer told his manager he was going to win the fight and his manager acceded. Confident in carrying the argument and the fight, Spencer threw a hook that was the finest of his career. The bell rang to signal the end of the round.

His alarm blared.

Spencer continued his hook, and his arm was parallel to the wall of his bedroom. Was an expert punch with force behind it, and Spencer had never thrown such a punch in his life.

For that moment of waking, Spencer was a boxer continuing his fight, and only in the next moment did Spencer remember being himself.

# Appomattox Courthouse

I am a man who is walking home from Appomattox Courthouse. My country is behind me. My home is in front of me. I am a man who has outlived his country.

The better number of fingers of my right hand are gone along with my country. I left them with the Confederacy like a keepsake. I learnt how to load and fire with what I had left and to use a pen to maintain my correspondence while the post still carried.

I am not a man lacking in education, though it has done me little good so far as it fed my romantic convictions. It might be averred that my education has done me great harm. Though many arrived at my youthful position and believed themselves Cavaliers without the year or so of college, having only thumbed through Sir Walter Scott, others, and lesser positioned still, managed the trick only on hearing the idea of a Cavalier, and a cause, and of Jeb Stuart with an ostrich feather in his cap.

Jeb Stuart is dead with his ostrich feather.

So is Stonewall, under the shade of the trees. The Marble Man is alive. General Lee signed the surrender and the country with it. He had greatly aged over the course of the late conflict, from its start until its end, cracks and dullness appearing in his marble.

I have aged as well, though I have not seen my likeness reflected with exactness since the loss of my compact. I have seen my visage doubled in those who have become aged alongside me, all become aged together like wearied doppelgängers in tattered gray. I know that I am no longer young with more certainty than might be communicated by vision alone.

It is a feeling in my nerves, such nerves as are still left to me, a great untightening of the strength of them and a dissipation of that strength. Perhaps that feeling is also the hunger that has carried away the muscle and the fat from my frame and left me lean and rawboned. I was stout and of ample proportion in the days of my youth and there were prognostications I would run to fat and corpulence in the fullness of my years and enjoyment of my inheritance.

I am walking to see what remains of my inheritance. The chattel have been manumitted and with them the bulk of the capital. A peculiar way of achieving total loss, what a wit might describe as a Republican depreciation.

I was to inherit the real estate as well as personal property and if the home was not burnt there might be a roof and a bed, the mattress stuffed with down or currency seeking a more profitable use, and the library which will be some pleasant distraction if not raided for kindling. The acreage might be cultivated still, and perhaps I will learn to pick cotton like a field hand how I relearnt to write like a man of education and breeding. And, if not cotton for lack of hands or markets, perhaps potatoes and greens, because as my country was reminded with increasing and deadening frequency during the late conflict, cotton is hard for the eating.

There were men with me at the beginning and they had the fortune of living nearer to the surrender. There are men who have passed me and who have conversed with me, and among them were men of the better sort of breeding and others who were my lessers in the antebellum, and we walked and conversed in the universal and leveled brotherhood of defeated men. There were others who I have passed and we have kept our mutual silence, and that silence was likewise an expression of the strange fraternity of the dispossessed of which we have become members by hard dues.

I have far to walk, and the narrow road to the Deep South is hardly better than a track. There is a ditch beside and below the track. There is a man in the ditch. There is a turkey vulture on the man in the ditch, and many flies. The mud in the ditch has coated the man's face so that if it was fired in a kiln like clay it would manufacture a death mask. The ditch is all mud and I have been walking through mud and the mud has coated my feet.

It has rained of late, and when it rained, I kept on through the rain until the rain became too heavy and the mud too soft. Then I sat beneath the trees and tried to rest under what cover they gave to me. The rain had a pleasant sound, though it would have been better to have been within my home or under the ground to listen to it.

I have become a man much accustomed to the rain. The rain was worse than the cold to live in, or the heat to fight in. It made the Virginia clay bad to fight in. The sacred soil of our land was not accommodating to us. I lost my shoes at New Market in the mud.

It broke many of our health. Condemned men to shivering malarial death.

And yet it is still pleasant to hear the rain.

The man had disappeared from my vision before the turkey vulture such that I could not have seen him, but I could very well see the top half of the bird busying itself in the ditch. Why I turned back my head, knowing I could see but only the turkey vulture, and that the presumptive object of my turning was another member of the unknown and unburied dead to which I have become much accustomed if never reconciled, is a consideration that has occupied my mental faculties and carried my frame many miles.

Perhaps to see Death one more time, for fear that too great a familiarity with him has left me indifferent. Like an Oriental Lamaist whose thoughts are turned constantly to death such that he might defeat himself and thereby find himself having defeated death.

I had Schopenhauer in the German, though my facility with the language is not so prodigious. And with him a fatalistic atheism, though I have come to accept the merit of a faith that can claim the death of death by forthcoming intervention of an external power.

I have not, though, yet accepted the Gospel, and my baptism possesses such claim for my soul upon the Heavenly Host as an unwitting infant's unwelcomed immersion might carry when unaccompanied by election. Though the matter of my election or pre-natal condemnation is, as the Reformers and presbyters explain, unknowable in life, and while its inerrancy and implacability appeal to me as a man whose pretended philosophy and constrained natural learning encourage him to believe the world inclines to predetermination by a harsh will, no experience in my years has led me to believe myself among those saints guaranteed a place near to the distant God of my upbringing.

What I have learnt and learnt dear has not inclined me to theology, or to Germans, although it owes something to the idea of the great and terrible Will.

Life has much blood in it.

I have done my share of the bleeding.

My country has bled white and dead.

I had reached South Carolina where Sherman had destroyed the rice fields and the mansions with his hard hand of war when my perspective began its change, subtle and deep. I was following the tracks of Sherman who had brought the North with him from Atlanta to the sea and then at the sea he had turned into the Carolinas because he couldn't burn the sea, though if it had been Confederate, he would have tried. Though I could not wish the man good health, I could respect a soul who understood that war was cruelty without trepidation. He was a man of the will, as was our general, though plebeian in affect and breeding, whereas General Lee was aristocratic. And Sherman had been victorious in war, whereas our General had been victorious merely in battle.

The mansion must have been grand and fine when it had all of it sides. The roof had fallen in. The columns were the color of burnt whitewash and the gashes in them showed hollow wood imitating marble.

My country had been of that sort, Corinthian columns made of hollow wood with master and his kin inside and fields around them and chattel. Our cause will be judged as unrighteous for this spirit, which was our despotic and republican freedom.

The master and his kin had fled elsewhere, perhaps to extended relations, somewhere Union armies had not reached. Or perhaps to roadside graves. It is a matter of one's predisposition to the sanguinary or the melancholic temperament, which end seemed the likelier.

There were Negroes in the shacks behind the big house. Some had likely taken to the road. They had hurried toward emancipation instead of waiting for it to meet them.

Perhaps they had reached it. Like the fate of their former masters, it is a matter of temperament. One who remained was sitting idle in the doorframe of his shack. I walked to him to inquire if there was a well from which I might draw water, or stores of food that might be distributed to a stranger in need.

I waited for the Negro to answer me and did not have the means to compel his answer. I realized as he sat with his face partially in the sun that his face was cleaner than mine, and that the South of my birth was dead.

Perhaps we would in the coming years return to something reminiscent of the old hierarchy between the races for which I shall not apologize. But the old order had its throat slit and like the Jacobinical French who had condemned one king to the guillotine and who had witnessed his brother's ineffectual restoration, though the ancient manner of things might be reimposed it could not be entirely restored. What had been an organic relationship between the higher and the lesser, a despotism certainly but a despotism on which an aristocratic freedom could flourish, could never replant itself once it had first been uprooted from its ancient soil.

What came after was like a potted plant transferred into a field. Though on external observance it might appear as native to its place, a man digging would find shallow and vulnerable roots.

But perhaps that was in the manner of the will that must devour all things. Is revolution not another kind of devouring?

From the Negro, I was eventually given permission to use the well though the question of food remained unanswered. I was uncomplaining for I had not expected water and it would have been an easy thing to deny me, or even to kill me.

I drew the water and the drawing tested my strength. I drank my fill and the water was stone cool and some relief, for though water was not over scarce how food was, cool water was a rarity to me and a palliative to the heat of walking. I filled my canteen and passed the permissive Negro's shack.

Taken by an impulse no less than my need to turn back to see the carrion-eater many miles before, I turned to the Negro with a great compulsion to ask of him what bore strange weight upon me.

Where has your master gone?

Massah's gone.

Where has he gone?

Gone south.

Why has massah gone to the South?

Place for him to go.

Why have you stayed?

Don't got any place else to be.

He reclined himself further into the darkness of the shack.

Much has left me of my time wandering after the surrender, but that short exchange has remained to me with great clarity. For I considered, as I resumed my walk, un-victualed but with a flask of well water and to such an extent the better provisioned, that the question resounded in my mind like a strange Oriental riddle.

Why has massah gone to the South?

I was along the trails of the Appalachian interior. I could not tell you why I took this farther route, dangerous and Unionist, except that I needed the elevation. God revealed Himself, or so the Old Testament recorded, on Mount Sinai, and though I am not such a man as can accept the scripture as Holy Writ, the divinity inhabits higher elevations. There is Burke's sublimity in them.

The trails, no better than logging paths, were deep and green. The switchbacks in the trails were such that each led only to further undifferentiated trails, surrounded by trees and the season was the high green and ferns along and over the paths. The air thinning with the height and the mobile wall of green was first numbing, and then took onto itself a strange character. The undifferentiated green, each turn in the path the same as the turn before, and my lungs not filling as deep as they were used to in their lowland condition, created in me a sensation not unlike the eating of opium, as I have read that narcotic described in firsthand accounts.

The effect was initially soporific, but with my senses removed from the meaningful differentiation of external stimulant, it was as though my cognition were forced to turn upon itself. Considering itself as though in a clean mirror in the back recesses and empty spaces of my mind.

Reflected in itself, I saw the question.

Why has massah gone to the South?

And with the question, and the elevation, and the perfection of the air and the clearing of consciousness, came an answer repeating.

Because it is in the nature of massah to have gone to the South.

Oceanic, a kind of grand vista, Balboa's first sighting of the Pacific. But it was of a kind of obscurity with its grandeur, as I could no more elucidate the answer that was presenting itself in my emptied mind than I could have discerned the cause behind the question's persistence.

It took much farther walking, reaching to the highest elevations, and arriving upon a clearing at the apex of the mountain such that the trees were spread before me, extending to the horizon like a green sea with leaves rustling like wave tips in the wind, that the answer took such form in my mind as might with difficulty be communicable.

In the unfolding of the necessity of massah's nature, he has always gone to the South. And in the unfolding of the necessity of the Negro's nature, he has always remained. And in the unfolding of the necessity of my nature, I have always walked a winding trail of defeat.

I knew that I had always walked the labyrinthine greenness of these paths, and seen the Negro lolling in the shack behind the dead mansion, and the dead man with his turkey vulture. That the General always surrendered, that Appomattox Courthouse was always the site of the Confederacy's grave. That Chancellorsville was always a victory, and Stonewall always dead on the shore.

All occurred as to their natures.

I had Leibniz by way of a commentary, and his monad which has no window into itself and yet acts in accord with itself is the nearest and barest approximation of this metaphysic known to me from a source other than my own intuition. The centrality of an undifferentiated and indivisible particle, from which arises differentiated and divisible beings all organized by a grand consciousness.

But as I descended from that great elevation my physical decline corresponded to a spiritual leveling, a dampening of enthusiasm, for man is not meant to remain permanently at such a high pitch. I had known war, and had been wounded, and seen other men die grievously, and the benignity of this conception though of great attraction to me and even possessing a kind of compulsion at that highest point, could no more lastingly take possession of me than could my Romantic sensibilities, my Christianity, or my Schopenhauer. Though, like those earlier convictions, this one stranger and harder classified, imprinted itself upon my nerves and left a deeper and fuller trace.

I was back along the lowlands and was nearing my destination. The fields that had once been familiar were cast in a burnt chiaroscuro whose material was the charcoaled remnants of timber and cropland and Southland.

I first began to see individuals familiar to me from my youth. Negroes of both sexes who had remained and, among the whites, women and those whose adolescence or disfigurement had spared them conscription or volunteerism. Some of the whites recognized me and called my name, and I spoke with them and nothing was offered. I knew it would be a hungry winter and without charity.

The sun had become large at the horizon and red when I reached the home of my youth. I had already been told of its fate and so shock was denied to me. The pillars had survived, and little else.

Instead of shock, the void of my consciousness was filled with wonder.

Had the ruin been in some distant Attica, it would have conveyed sublimity in its defeat fit for the walls of a grand salon. A lithograph of the scene would have made permanent its transient and ravished beauty. Each perspective as appropriate to the media.

I suppose that from the perspective of the divinity or the grand consciousness, as I understood those things at the highest point of my journey, that wonder and sublimity and beauty were all experienced singularly and all exist continuously in some state denied to my own consciousness. But those must also coincide with the ruin, and the ruins in the more prosaic and ordinary sense of things were what remained to me after that initial vision.

Those of my kin still living had been reduced to a hastily and shoddily constructed cabin. My sisters and a brother whose voice had not yet broken, and so was still intact in his entirety. They greeted me with greater or lesser enthusiasm dependent upon their particular natures and the extent of their hunger, though the expressions of love were sincere.

They slept in one room, and the room was poisonous with vapors from the stove and brutal with the heat. They had once each had their own feather bed, and now it was the sickliest and weakest who had a shared camp bed. The rest shared an earthen floor.

It had not been to them to flee, but it had been to them to live in a manner much reduced. It became apparent by negative inference that my parents were not among them.

Where have my parents gone?

They have gone beneath the ground.

How did they die?

Typhoid and Yankee troops.

Both killed them?

Typhoid killed Mother and Yankee troops shot Father.

Why was I not told?

They died after the mail stopped carrying.

Where can they be found?

They can be found beneath the disturbed earth behind this cabin.

My surviving kin waited for me to make my visitation. I walked out behind the cabin and in the dying light saw the earth darkened and with only scrubby grass and weeds in two sections approximating rectangles, one the longer and one the shorter.

I took a place on the earthen floor and slept. I was possessed of the impression, in the disorientation accompanying proximity to sleep, that I was continuous with the earth beneath me and extended to my parents entombed within it, and that I encompassed them and made their tomb into a shelter.

From there, the semi-lucidity of my near dreaming extended farther, extending so far as to all the bodies buried south of the Mason-Dixon Line, and farther still along the underground trails of the dead to our salient that ended at Gettysburg. And not only underground, but those still resting upon it, and I was with what was left of the man in the ditch after the turkey buzzard and time. We were one and there was a comfort in this identification with a bare skull wearing a muddy death mask, and many others bleached or rotten.

All the citizens of the Republic of the Dead, and I, like Leviathan, was composed of them.

On waking, I briefly thought myself the consul of a defeated land.

The Negroes had mostly remained though manumitted, and the landless whites who had tenanted outlying fields. My family retained title to the land, and though un-probated it had passed to me by instrument of my father. I had returned to discover myself the county's wealthiest man, though that meant little more than a kind of propertied penury.

On such a bedrock our future prosperity would have to rest. We were a grand family once, and though we should not attain such grandeur again we might have sustenance and even some niggling prosperity.

After waking and learning of my new fortune, and walking my bare fields, I planted a marker on the graves of my parents.

With their marker was recognition that we had been liberated from our struggle. Freedom has been forced upon us. A freedom of Negro slaves and planter aristocrats ended at Appomattox, and a new freedom has descended upon us from the North.

Perhaps this is not the Will, though it is accompanied with much bleeding. The world must end and those left after the end must continue, and so the world must begin again. A kind of transmigration of the world by stubborn inertia.

But though I have outlived my country, and many years shall pass, I am still a man walking home from Appomattox Courthouse. I shall be walking the remainder of my days, and into eternity.

# ACKNOWLEDGMENTS

Writers steal from their own lives and the lives of others, and I am particularly indebted to a group of friends that I have made over the last several years. In the interest of anonymity, I have to thank using generic language, which comes nowhere close to expressing my gratitude. They have made my life something better than what it was, and richer, and some of them might recognize their own lines of dialogue spoken in passing or as part of long conversations that made their way into this collection.

Thanks also to everyone at Passage Publishing, particularly Lomez, for reaching out to an unknown writer, and to my editor, whose work on this collection has made it something to be proud of. A book has many parents, and this collection would not exist without the support of everyone at Passage who has had a hand in its production.

This book is dedicated in memory of my grandmother, who exposed me to far too much concerning religion and religious thought far too early in life, and for whom I am eternally grateful. I would not be the person I am today if not for her influence, and her love. I miss her every day, and hope this book can be a token of my memory of her. She would not have liked this book, but she would have pretended to, and nothing more can be asked from a grandmother than that. I would also like to thank my grandfather, who was the first person to know about this collection, and who kept my confidences during the long period of writing it.

V.N. EBERT's debut story "Georgia Buddha" won the first Passage Prize for Fiction and was published in *Passage Prize: Volume 1* in 2022. He was also featured in the Passage Publishing anthology *After the War*. His work has appeared in *Man's World* and *Apocalypse Confidential*. Selections of his work can be found on his website: www.vnebert.com.